Hood Riley
and the
Ice Man

MALLORY MONROE

*This novel is a work of fiction. All
characters are fictitious. Any similarities to
anyone living or dead are completely
accidental. The specific mention of known
places or venues are not meant to be exact
replicas of those places, but they are purposely
embellished or imagined for the story's sake.
The cover art are models. They are not actual*

characters.

THE RAGS TO ROMANCE SERIES

STANDALONE BOOKS

IN PUBLICATION ORDER:

1. BOBBY SINATRA: IN ALL THE WRONG PLACES

2. BOONE & CHARLY: SECOND CHANCE LOVE

3. PLAIN JANE EVANS AND THE BILLIONAIRE

4. GENTLEMAN JAMES AND GINA

5. MONTY & LaSHAY: RESCUE ME

6. TONY SINATRA: IF LOVING YOU IS WRONG

7. WHEN A MAN LOVES A WOMAN

8. THE DUKE AND THE MAID

9. BOONE AND CHARLY: UPSIDE DOWN LOVE

10. HOOD RILEY AND THE ICE MAN

11. RECRUITED BY THE BILLIONAIRE

12. ABANDONED HEARTS

MALLORY MONROE SERIES:

THE RENO GABRINI/MOB BOSS SERIES (22 BOOKS)

THE SAL GABRINI SERIES (12 BOOKS)

THE TOMMY GABRINI SERIES (11 BOOKS)

THE MICK SINATRA SERIES (15 BOOKS)

THE BIG DADDY SINATRA SERIES (7 BOOKS)

THE TEDDY SINATRA SERIES (5 BOOKS)

THE TREVOR REESE SERIES (3 BOOKS)

THE AMELIA SINATRA SERIES (2 BOOKS)

THE BRENT SINATRA SERIES (1 BOOK)

THE ALEX DRAKOS SERIES (9 BOOKS)

THE OZ DRAKOS SERIES (2 BOOKS)

THE MONK PALETTI SERIES (2 BOOKS)

THE PRESIDENT'S GIRLFRIEND SERIES (8 BOOKS)

THE PRESIDENT'S BOYFRIEND SERIES (1 BOOK)

THE RAGS TO ROMANCE SERIES (12 BOOKS)

STANDALONE BOOKS:

ROMANCING MO RYAN

MAEBELLE MARIE

LOVING HER SOUL MATE

LOVING THE HEAD MAN

TABLE OF CONTENTS

PROLOGUE

CHAPTER ONE

CHAPTER TWO

CHAPTER THREE

CHAPTER FOUR

CHAPTER FIVE

CHAPTER SIX

CHAPTER SEVEN

CHAPTER EIGHT

CHAPTER NINE

CHAPTER TEN

CHAPTER ELEVEN

CHAPTER TWELVE

CHAPTER THIRTEEN

CHAPTER FOURTEEN

CHAPTER FIFTEEN

CHAPTER SIXTEEN

CHAPTER SEVENTEEN

CHAPTER EIGHTEEN

CHAPTER NINETEEN

CHAPTER TWENTY

CHAPTER TWENTY-ONE

CHAPTER TWENTY-TWO

CHAPTER TWENTY-THREE

CHAPTER TWENTY-FOUR

CHAPTER TWENTY-FIVE

CHAPTER TWENTY-SIX

CHAPTER TWENTY-SEVEN

CHAPTER TWENTY-EIGHT

CHAPTER TWENTY-NINE

CHAPTER THIRTY

CHAPTER THIRTY-ONE

CHAPTER THIRTY-TWO

CHAPTER THIRTY-THREE

CHAPTER THIRTY-FOUR

EPILOGUE

PROLOGUE

SEVENTEEN YEARS EARLIER

Young Maxwell Cassidy opened the front door at his parents' home with a grin on his face and joy in his heart. The gorgeous girl he loved to mess around with every time he was home from college smiled back at him. And when he grabbed her by the arm and pulled her across the threshold, kissing on her before he even closed the door, she went along with his frat-boy boorishness. Because Breena Novak knew exactly what she was getting with Max Cassidy. She was young and black and relied on her great looks to win the attention of men, and he was the super-fine son of a millionaire who let the good times roll. It was all fun and games for him, and she knew it.

But in the three years they'd been hanging out, she'd grown to love him.

But she also knew Max had a reckless streak about him. He could get away with a slap on the wrist for something her black ass would do serious time in prison over. She pulled back from him. "What about your parents?" she asked him. "I'm not trying to get into any trouble with your parents."

"Out to dinner," Max said, barely able to speak as he was kissing her on her ears, her cheek, her long, dark neck as if he couldn't get enough of her. "I told you that when we talked on the phone."

"But when will they be back, Max?" Breena lifted her chin to give him full access to her neck because she was enjoying it too. "It doesn't take all night to eat no dinner."

"It'll be a couple hours at least," Max said, nearly out of breath. "They're out with a group of their friends." Then he added *"just relax"* in the softest of voices, and kept going strong.

At twenty-two, Breena was only a year younger than Max, but she was used to being with much older men. But what Max lacked in experience, he made up in vigor. He was the best man she'd ever been with in every way. That was why she was wrapping her arms around his neck as they began kissing passionately on the lips. That was why she was panting just as hard as Max was and couldn't wait to have him inside of her.

Max first saw Breena when she was a server at a local bar. They slept together that same night and became fast lovers. And even now, in his second year of law school, she was the only girl he wanted to be with whenever he was home from college. He knew she had sugar daddies left and right, all of whom together barely managed to give her a decent living. But Max never gave her a dime and she kept coming back to him. He prided himself on that.

And he couldn't delay a second longer. He swept her up into his arms, kicked the door shut and locked it, and began carrying her across the foyer toward the stairs so ready to put it on her he could hardly contain himself, when he heard that familiar, annoying voice.

"*Maxwell*?"

Max and Breena quickly stopped kissing and both turned in the direction of the tiny sound. When Breena saw that it was the little blue-eyed girl she knew to be Max's three-year-old sister, she couldn't believe it. "Your baby sister's here? Really, Max?" Breena displayed her own level of annoyance. How could they do anything with a little girl in the house?

Max just wanted to get Bree upstairs. He sat her back on her feet. "What is it, Jen?" he asked his kid sister with impatience in his voice. "Can't you see I'm busy? I told you not to bother me girl!"

"I can't find my Barbie," Jen complained.

"Which one? You literally have thousands of them."

"The blue one," said Jen.

That was a new one on Breena. They were just beginning to make black barbies. "A blue Barbie?" she asked.

"She came in a blue dress," Max explained. "Did you look in the cedar chest where the rest of them are?" he asked Jen.

But Jen nodded so forcefully that her blonde candy curls whipped back and forth like they could hurt somebody. "She's not in there."

Max exhaled. "Wait here," he said as he hurried to the kitchen.

Jen stared at Breena the whole time. Breena smiled at the nosy little brat, and tried to make small talk, but Jen just kept staring at her.

Max returned quickly with an ice cream bar. When Jen saw it, her eyes lit up like lasers and she excitedly reached for it.

But Max pulled it back out of her reach. "You promise to stay in the play room and play with your other barbies until I can find the blue one?"

Jen nodded her head energetically. She only had eyes for that ice cream. And as soon as Max gave it to her, she happily went back into the play room, skipping as she went, and Max closed the door behind her.

"You didn't tell me you were babysitting," Breena said.

"You didn't ask," Max said. "But forget all

of that," he added as he grabbed Breena by the hand this time and began running with her up the stairs. Breena started laughing at his desperation, and he was grinning too.

But when he got her in his bedroom and threw her on his bed, their amusement was overtaken by an entirely different emotion. And when Max began kissing her again, and then lifting her blouse and bra and kissing her breasts, there was no longer any smiles on Breena's face. And her own desperation began to show.

And by the time Max had lifted her skirt, excited that she wore no underwear, and pulled down his own pants, they were at that stage of no return.

When Max entered her, she thought she was ready for that entrance. But like always whenever they did their thing, it was more than she expected. His massive size, and the way he thrust himself inside of her without any pretense of taking it easy on her, always gave her such a jolt that it kept her on a high the entire time he was inside of her.

Max was pumping his ass off. The bed was bouncing he was pumping so hard. Breena was scratching him and letting out yelps of joy he was pumping so hard. Sweat was pouring as he pumped.

And when she finally climaxed, she buried her nails so deeply into his back and lifted up to him as if she couldn't bear how wonderful he was putting it on her, that it made him cum too.

Breena was Max's gold standard. No other girl turned him on the way she did, which made his climaxes with her so electrifying. He was leaned over, calling her name, as he came.

And after they both were well spent, and Max was adoring her smooth, dark-chocolate face and big, golden-brown eyes, he knew that no other girl could possibly be more beautiful than Bree. He could fall hard for her and he knew it.

But it wasn't possible. She was not of their social status. He fall for anybody deemed beneath that status and his parents, who already knew he seemed to favor black girls over all others, warned him in no uncertain terms. He could have his black girls all he wanted. They had no issue with that. But those girls had better be on-par-with or above his own social status. There was no other way around it. But that couldn't stop his feelings.

He kissed Breena on the lips once again, and then eased out of her.

Breena knew her feelings for Max were going nowhere. He'd already told her not to fall for him. He'd already told her it would only be for fun and to never take their get-togethers seriously. She told him she never did, but she was lying. From the moment she laid eyes on that big hunk of flesh called Maxwell Cassidy, she was smitten. She knew even then that he'd be the love of her life.

But that was why it was always painful when they had to part. That was why she never wanted him to have to throw her out.

As soon as Max got off of her, and laid on his back beside her, she didn't hesitate. She began getting up.

Max reached for her arm to pull her back against him because he didn't want it to end either, but Breena pulled away from him. "Gotta go," she said.

"Why?"

Breena began putting her clothes back in place. "You know why."

"One of your sugar daddies waiting for you?"

Breena didn't respond to that.

"Why must you have sugar daddies anyway? I told you I'm rich."

"Your father is rich," Breena said. "You're a broke-ass college student."

Max laughed.

Then Breena stood up and looked at him.

At his dick first, and then at his gorgeous face. Why did she always fall for the worst possible guys? "Walk me downstairs," she said.

Max got out of bed, arranged his own clothing, and then began walking with her downstairs.

"As soon as I graduate and earn my own money," he said the way he was always saying to her, "I'll set you up in your own apartment, get you a car. The whole nine, okay? Just don't do anything drastic like marrying one of those jokers."

Breena looked at Max as they walked down the winding staircase of his parents' home. "So what are you saying? You're going to marry me?" She already knew the answer.

Max hated that the answer was a resounding no, because he really liked Bree more than any other girl he'd ever been with. But his life was his life. He didn't know any other way to live. "I told you the deal. We aren't going around that mulberry bush again. I'm just saying if you're going to have a sugar daddy, let it be me."

Breena's heart dropped. How could he think any woman would find such an awful thing appealing? *If you're going to be a hoe, be my hoe*, was what he was saying. But that was Max. She either had to take his scraps or take none of him.   She wished she was strong enough to take none. But she wasn't.

She leaned over and kissed him on the lips.   Which caused him to grab her as they stood on those stairs and kiss her with a long, endearing kiss again. And then they kept on walking.

"Who's the guy this week?" Max asked her as they walked.

But Breena suddenly stopped in her tracks, causing Max to bump into her.

He looked at her, wondering if she was about to tell him something profound about her latest sugar daddy. "What is it?"

"Are your parents back already?"

Max frowned. "No way. I told you it would be a couple hours before they got back. Why do you keep bringing them up?"

"Because," Breena said, and motioned her head.

Max looked where she was looking, and when he saw that his front door was wide open, he frowned.

"Did you leave the door open like that?" Breena, confused, asked.

"No," Max said, as confused as she was, and began running down the stairs past her. She ran behind him.

But as he was approaching the door, his

heart dropped. And when he saw that the playroom door was wide open, too, when he knew he'd shut that door as well, he ran into the playroom calling out his sister's name. "Jennifer?" he called out as he ran in. "Jen?" But Jen wasn't there.

And when he didn't see her, a kind of dread came over him that caused his heart to start hammering. His sister never broke promises. Never! But when he saw that her ice cream cone was on the floor of her playroom, melted into a puddle of chocolate, he knew something awful had happened. Jen would have never ran outside and left her beloved ice cream. Never!

He ran out of the playroom, knocking Breena aside, and out of the front door.

Breena glanced into the playroom too. When she saw the melted ice cream on the floor, and no Jen, she knew what that meant too. What kid leaves ice cream behind? She ran behind Max.

But Max was already running around the big house on a street filled with big houses. "Stay here in case she comes back," he yelled at Breena as he ran to a few of those other houses asking his neighbors if they'd seen his baby sister. They all knew the Cassidy family. They were in their same social circle. But

17

nobody had seen Jen.

"Jen!" Max was screaming all over the neighborhood. "Jen! Jennifer!"

When he got back to the house, Breena had already called 911, and neighbors were already out of their homes and running to the Cassidy house, getting ready to form a search party too.

"Call my parents!" Max yelled to one of his neighbors with terror in his voice, as he ran to his Camaro and hopped inside. Breena wanted to go with him. She knew she couldn't hang around there. But he took off like a bat out of hell and left her behind. In search of his annoying, beloved sister. That guilt riding him like an all-wheel drive because somehow he knew, as he gripped that steering wheel and nearly crashed twice looking down side streets for her, that this was not going to end with some happy story about how she just so happened to wandered off to play that night. Jen wouldn't do something like that.

He searched until well after midnight. He could barely see the road in front of him, but he kept on searching. He drove up and down the same streets a hundred times searching. He drove around and around the same corners searching. No way was his sister going to appear on some damn milk carton. No way was his sister going to be lost forever. He kept on searching.

But she was nowhere to be found.

And when that reality sat in, it left him so empty, and so overwhelmed with grief, that he was beyond panicked.

But it was only the beginning of his troubles. Because as soon as he drove back home, his father came tearing out of the house, grabbed him just as his car door opened, and began beating him down right there on their driveway. He threw Max to the ground and was beating the life out of him. His father's neighbors and business partner and driver and other people Max didn't even know all were pulling and tugging and trying to wrestle him away from Max. They fell over pulling the big man off of Max.

But Max's father wasn't done with him yet. He got back up and hurried back for more. He was screaming at Max, blaming him for what happened to his precious little girl, as he bulldozed his way into Max, who was just getting back on his feet. He slammed Max back down onto their fancy pavers, and began beating him all over again. And when they pulled him up off Max again, he was kicking Max in the ribs, in the head, stomping on him like a dirty dog. And Max just laid there, balled up in a fetal position, and took every blow.

And when it was all over, and a bleeding Max was helped to his feet by his best friend Jason and Jason's parents, who were also in their social circle and had gathered at the house too, Max had a feeling unlike he'd ever felt before. As he watched his own parents look at him with nothing but contempt and hatred in their eyes, and such *pain*, Max knew. Somehow he instinctively that no matter what they tried to do to get her back, and no matter how far to the ends of the earth they were willing to go to find her, or how many years it took them to get there, he was never going to see his baby sister again. He would never be able to even acknowledge her existence, or say her name, ever again.

Somehow, within the very first hours of her disappearance, he already knew what the end was going to be.

CHAPTER ONE

SEVENTEEN YEARS LATER
PRESENT DAY

As soon as the jumbo jet landed and began taxing the runway of the private airfield, newlywed Hood Riley-Cassidy, along with her sister Rita and big brother Ricky, stepped out of Rita's Lexus to welcome Max back home. All three siblings had been hanging out together all day, and was having a late dinner at a local soul food restaurant when the call came in that Max was coming back to town a day earlier than anticipated, and that his private plane would be landing within the hour. There was no time to do anything else but to hop into Ricky's Jeep and get to the airfield.

But unbeknownst to them, Max's longtime driver Dobbs had already been ordered by Jason Bogart, Max's right-hand man, to get to the airfield, and Ricky's beloved but well-worn Jeep paled in comparison to that shiny black stretch limousine waiting for the boss.

And Max was definitely the boss. He employed Ricky and Rita within his corporation just after they reunited with their kid sister. They were trainees, and making low-grade trainee money for that first year, but they were grateful to finally have the kind of career path that before Max they could have only dreamed of having. They both also viewed Max with his domineering ways as Hood's boss too, but he wasn't. He was Hood's brand-new husband: a husband that returned from their honeymoon and had to immediately fly to Texas to take over some deadlocked, crucial negotiations. He'd been gone for nearly a week. She could hardly wait to see him again.

They walked over to the limo and spoke to Dobbs, but Rita was mostly trying to remind her younger sister to never cede all of her power to Max.

"You don't keep a man by treating him like he's a King," she said to Hood. "Act like you're the prize, not him, because guess what? You are the prize. Act like you can take him or leave him when he gets off that plane, because you can. Don't put that man on a pedestal."

Hood heard what her sister was saying, but she wasn't trying to hear it either. She wasn't trying to get marital advice from somebody like Rita, whose choice in men tended toward the abusive or the extremely abusive, and she'd never been married a day in her life. And for her to think that a woman like Hood, who didn't know the meaning of deception, was going to act as if she could take her husband or leave him after not feasting her eyes on him for nearly a week, was insanity. Rita didn't know what she was talking about. But Hood was never the kind of person to argue with people. She let them argue with themselves.

Ricky, however, had no such problem setting their sister straight. Of the three siblings, Ricky was the oldest and had been out of their lives the longest. But he and Hood were thick as thieves now, and he always had Hood's back. "You talking crazy, sis," he said to Rita.

"What's crazy about it?"

"How can you stand there and tell that girl to treat her husband like she can't stand the sight of him."

Rita was shocked. "That's not what I'm saying all at!"

"That's what you said."

"I said she can't let a man have power over her the way she's letting Max do her. Because he won't respect that in the end."

"Rita, please," said Ricky dismissively.

"Case in point," said Rita, determined to prove her point. "They just got back from their honeymoon. Just got back. And what does Max do? He takes off for a week!"

"He's running an empire," Hood reminded her big sister.

"Stop making excuses for him!" Rita fired back. "He needs to be here to show you how to manage in his world. I can't show you. Ricky sure as hell can't show you. What we know? We don't know shit either. But Max needs to be here to show you the ropes. I'm telling you to stop giving in to him so easily, and I'm not taking it back!"

Hood just stood there, dressed on full fleek in her form-fitting white dress and heels, with her red, short jacket thrown across her shoulders, looking nothing like that tomboyish girl she used to be. Max made certain his wife wasn't out there looking any kind of way, and Ricky and Rita both appreciated it. Because, they knew, leave it to Hood and she'd be in jeans and jerseys every day.

But Ricky also knew that Hood wasn't thinking about what Rita was saying. Even as a kid, Hood took her own counsel. Even as a kid, she did whatever the hell she thought was best for her, regardless of what others tried to tell her was best. She was standing there, looking at that plane, and she was thinking alright. But Ricky knew it had nothing to do with what Rita was talking about. Nobody was ever going to be handling Hood.

Except for Max. Ricky kind of agreed with Rita on that part. But the taking him or leaving him part? He wasn't down for that.

And Hood wasn't either. Because as soon as she saw Max step off of his private jet and began walking down those airstairs in his dark shades with his suit coat off and held up by his finger over his shoulder, looking so fine it reminded her how easily he turned her on when most men didn't even get a rise out of her, she wanted to jump for joy.

Even Rita had to acknowledge Max's commanding presence. "For a man his age, that's a good-looking white boy," she admitted.

"A man his age?" asked Ricky. "You talk like forty is ancient."

"It is when you're twenty-nine like Hood."

Ricky looked at Hood. "The last thing on her mind is that man's age," he said. "Believe that."

And as soon as Max's feet hit the ground and he began walking toward them, smiling when he saw his wife, Hood did as her body was threatening to do all along, and she jumped for joy.

"Don't do it, Hood," Rita warned her. "Don't you do it, girl."

But Hood did it. She took off running to

greet her husband.

Rita shook her head. "It's like talking to a brick wall. She didn't hear a word I said!"

"She heard every word you said," Ricky said. "She just can't be anybody but who she is. Just like you are. Just like I am. We aren't bougie people and we don't know how to be bougie. So just take a chill pill, sis. She got this. Hood ain't nobody's doormat."

"You could have fooled me," Rita said as Hood was still running to Max like a wild *banjee*. But what Rita didn't acknowledge was that Max was running to Hood, too, and smiling as if he was as happy to see her as she was to see him.

Because he was. Max loved Hood's authenticity. He loved how she never played games with him or tried to be anybody but who she was. And she loved him. There was no doubt in anybody's mind that Hood loved Max.

After his wife and child died in that plane he was piloting, he swore to never go down that matrimony road again. And then he met a girl named Hood who defied even the label her mother put on her and became the most ethical, trustworthy, and honest human being he'd ever met. That was why he broke his own ironclad rule and married her. That was why, when their bodies met on that tarmac and slammed against each other, he dropped his suit coat and pulled her into his arms. He'd missed her so much that it was painful. And despite all the eyes that might have been on them, he showed how much he missed her by lifting her off her feet, inhaling that intoxicatingly sweet fresh scent he loved to smell on her, and kissing her with an endearing, passionate kiss.

Marrying Hood did not come without blowback for Max. He was privately ostracized in his social circle and outwardly condemned by some. He was brutalized in the press for falling for a woman they felt was so beneath him that they took to calling her *Hood Rat* Riley. But he knew what gem he had. They could all kiss Max's ass. He knew Hood was head-and-shoulders above every single one of their critics.

And he kept on kissing her so passionate that even Ricky thought they needed to get a room. But then Max, who wasn't about to give anybody a reason to disparage Hood any further than they already had, placed her back on her feet, picked up his suit coat, kept his arm around her waist, and began walking with her to the limousine.

When they made it to the vehicles, he spoke to Ricky and Rita, talking with them mostly about their new jobs as trainees and how it was working out for them, and then Ricky and Rita said their goodbyes and got into Ricky's

Jeep. Max and Hood got into the limo. Dobbs closed them in, got in behind the wheel, and took off.

But Max was already kissing Hood passionately again as soon as they sat on that backseat. "I missed you so much," he was saying as he kissed her lips, and her tender cheeks, and her long, graceful neck. "You missed me?"

"Every second," said Hood, breathing heavily too. "I almost caught a bus to Arizona."

Max laughed. He loved this girl! But when he placed her on his lap, with her straddling him and facing him, all smiles were gone. He reached beneath her dress, ripped her panties open, and began fondling her. "Why didn't you come?" he asked as he watched her reaction to his fingers.

"I knew you were busy," said Hood breathlessly, reacting to his fingers.

"Wanna cum now?" he asked her. He felt her reaction to that question when her vagina began to pulsate against his fingers so intensely that no response was needed. He took control of her mouth again, kissing her hard as her wetness saturated his fingers. He unzipped his pants quickly, pulled out his fully aroused, rock-hard penis, and entered her with an agonizingly slow thrust that caused her to groan in his mouth.

And right there, in the backseat of that limousine, he started doing her.

Hood's eyes were nearly closed as he did her, as she felt the wonderment of his massive penis and his deep penetration inside of her.

They both were groaning as he did her, knowing Dobbs could hear them but unable to shut it down.

Hood leaned against Max, and hugged him tightly, and laid her head on his shoulder as he did her. He was lifting her ass up and down, and had her riding his cock so hard that he thought he was going to cum before they barely had gotten started. He loved how she made him feel!

Hood loved it, too, as he made her feel as if nothing else mattered to him except pleasing her.

Max's eyes were so hooded and his breath was so labored that he knew he was going to have a hard time handling his climax. But when Hood came and started trembling as she leaned her gorgeous neck back to enjoy the fullness of her cum, Max almost lost it. But when he started to feel how hard she was pulsating against his dick, and his dick was throbbing right back at her, he couldn't control himself a second longer.

He came too, with a cum that had him squeezing his dick as hard as he was squeezing her ass, and he poured all his love inside of her. He poured and he poured. Until he was poured out. Until he was so drained that he could hardly hold her up.

Then they looked at each other amazed again at how in sync they truly were. "Welcome back," Hood said to him. And he smiled, kissed her again, and held her even tighter.

And when they made it home, they were still so drained that they had only to get upstairs and fall into bed. And promptly fall asleep.

It was heavenly to Hood having Max's naked body lying beside her again, and holding her as they cuddled. And they remained that way for hours.

Until, just after eleven that night, Hood's cell phone rang.

When she saw that it was Rita, she looked to see if Max was still asleep. When she saw that he was still sound asleep, she eased out of bed and took the call in their bathroom.

But within seconds, and with no hesitation whatsoever, she was back in the bedroom dressing furiously.

CHAPTER TWO

The double doors of Max's mansion flew open and Hood hurried out, hopped into her Mercedes convertible Max had purchased for her, and sped around the horseshoe driveway heading straight for the gate. By the time she arrived, gate security had already opened it wide and she was able to drive straight through without breaking her speed. All because Rita had phoned crying hysterically and yelling profanities about some dude Hood had never heard of before. It was all so unlike Rita that it was scaring Hood.

That was why she couldn't get to her sister fast enough. She was speeding in and out of lanes getting there. They had only recently been reunited after over a decade apart. But thanks to Max, she and her siblings, along with her nephew Tim, were all together again. And all four of them made a pact to never leave each other, and to always have each other's back. But that went without saying for Hood.

When she finally made it to Rita's house, she was glad to see Ricky's Jeep already there. But the fact that their big brother was already there only heightened Hood's anxiety. She parked across the bottom of the driveway and jumped out. Although it was chilly out, she had thrown on a pair of shorts and a Bears jersey to get there. But as she ran to the front door, she was too concerned about her sister to even feel the cold.

The door was unlocked and she hurried inside. The first thing Hood saw was the condition of the house. Tables and chairs were overturned. Vases and lamps were busted and lying on the floor. And blood was on that floor.

But when Hood saw that Rita was lying on the sofa and Ricky was seated beside her, her heart dropped. She hurried to her sister.

When she saw the condition of her sister's face, that it was swollen and bruised and Ricky was compressing a heavy cloth on her arm, as if it had been bleeding, Hood dropped to her knees at the side of the sofa.

Rita, knowing how her kid sister had always been a worrier, attempted to reassure her. "It's alright, Hood. I'm okay."

"But what happened?" Hood was still

trying to take in all that she was seeing. Especially her sister's battered face.

"I told you over the phone. Me and this dude got into it."

Hood frowned. "What dude?"

"You don't know him."

"Some white dude named Sonny," Ricky said. "I met him before."

"And he beat you like this?" Hood asked her. *And you let him*, she wanted to ask her.

"I beat his ass too. It wasn't just him."

"But he walked away and you're laying up here needing to go to the hospital."

"I ain't going to no hospitals! You know how I feel about those places."

Hood understood that. She hated them too. "Where was Timmy when all of this was happening?"

"Tim is a grown-ass man who met some fast-tail girl he's been laying up with. He's never here anymore."

Hood exhaled. "So what are we gonna do about it?" she asked.

"That's what I wanna know," said Ricky. "Ain't no way this fool getting away with this."

"Who said anything about him getting away with it?" Rita was defiant too. "I'm gonna kick his ass, that's what I'm gonna do. And y'all gonna help me."

"Damn right we are," said Ricky.

"Damn straight," agreed Hood.

Where they came from that was how it was done. Somebody got the best of you, it went without saying that you get your posse together and get the best of them. Consequences? They worried about that later. "But you aren't in any condition to kick anybody's anything," Hood added. "Me and Ricky will handle this situation."

"Just tell us where we can find him," said Ricky.

"Y'all going now?"

Ricky looked at Rita. Their oddball mother thought it was cute to have her first two children with RR as their initials, as if they were going to be as close as their names. But it wasn't the case. He and Rita generally bumped heads, mainly because of Rita's bossiness. Ricky and Hood were the close ones. "No, Rita, we're going next month," he responded to her. "Why wouldn't we go now? What you want that bastard to get away? What if he leaves town, Reet? That's gonna be okay with you?"

Rita shook her head. "No. The way he held me down and was punching me like I was a dude he was punching? No way he's getting away with what he did to me. I fought back but he was so big. Then he started choking me like

34

he wanted to kill me. And he would have choked me out if I hadn't grabbed that lamp and hit him upside his big-ass head. Then he spit on me like I was lower than a dog to him." Tears reappeared in her swollen eyes. "Like I was nothing to him."

Ricky and Hood glanced at each other as if they were more convinced than ever that they were going to get this dude.

"And you know the worst part about it?" asked Rita.

"There's worse than what you already told us?"

"I thought we had something beautiful going on," said Rita. "I thought he could be the one you know? That's how pathetic I've become about these damn men. I'm thinking a guy who almost killed me might have been the one." She shook her head again. "No. His ass ain't getting away."

"Where he live at?" asked Ricky. "Just give us his address and we'll do the rest."

"You know where that trailer park on Balinstone is?"

Ricky was surprised. "He lives over *there*?"

"What's wrong with over there?" asked Hood. She didn't know that area at all.

"You thought a white boy that lives in that

hellraising trailer park over on Balinstone could be the one? Now come on, Reet!" Ricky was staring at her with astonishment on his handsome face. What happened to his confident, self-assured sister in all those years he was out of her life? This was so not Rita!

Rita looked away. Because she knew her desperation was showing.

Hood knew it too. But Rita was just like their mother used to be when it came to men. She always had to have one, no matter how lowdown dirty dog they were. Hood was just the opposite.

She stood up. "Which trailer is his?" she asked Rita.

"As soon as you drive in, take a hard left and keep going down that side road. You'll find his trailer in the back all by itself. You can't miss it. He owns that whole section back there."

"Any animals?"

"Not that I've ever seen."

Hood looked at her. "Not that you've ever seen? Looks like you'd know that, Rita. How long have you known this joker?"

"A few days," said Ricky. "And she already had him moved in."

Rita frowned. "That's a lie! His ass got his own place. What I look like moving him into mine?"

"He was acting like he was moved in when I saw him over here," said Ricky. "He had the nerve to answer my sister's door and ask me what I want. Like it's his crib and I'm bothering him. I almost kicked his ass right then and there."

But Hood was still trying to understand her sister. "But how could you let him be spending the night at your house when you just met him a few days ago?"

"You let Max spend the night with you when you barely knew him. At least I knew *of* Sonny before we hooked up like that. Your ass didn't know shit about Max."

That wasn't true. Max was the man who had purchased the restaurant Hood was working in when she lived in Utah, and his plan was to convert it into yet another one of his gazillion Cassbars. He promptly fired Hood because she didn't have that certain look he was going for. She didn't look like a hoe, was how Hood felt about it.

And that wasn't her only knowledge of Max before they officially met either. She saved him from a carjacking at a gas station weeks before that. She knew a whole lot more about Max than Rita apparently knew about that Sonny character. But Hood wasn't the kind of person to argue with people. "Let's go get this dude," she said to Ricky.

"Keep this on that arm," said Ricky as he placed Rita's other hand on the heavy cloth.

"It isn't bleeding anymore," Rita said as she took over the compress duties.

"And we don't want it to start bleeding again. Just keep it there."

And then Ricky and Hood began to head toward the front door.

"Hood?" Rita knew, between the two of her siblings, which one was more gangster.

Hood turned around. "Yeah?"

"Beat his ass for me. And make sure he knows y'all there for me."

Hood nodded. "Don't worry. He already got his ass-kicking in. We're gonna get ours in now."

Ricky nodded at that too, and they left, locking the door behind them.

But Rita, overwhelmed with anger, pain, and *sadness*, just started crying again.

CHAPTER THREE

Max turned over onto his back and then his eyes opened. The room was dark, which meant no light at all was penetrating through the floor-to-ceiling curtainless windows. Which meant it was still nighttime, or early morning. He didn't know which.

He grabbed for his cell phone on his night stand and glanced at the time. Eleven-forty-two.

He had just gotten back in town around seven that night, after a business trip to Arizona, and had carried Hood upstairs, fully expecting to finish what they had started in the limousine. But as soon as his head laid on that pillow, he knew it wasn't going to be happening. He was just too tired. He held her in his arms, and they chatted for a few minutes, but it didn't take much longer than that for him to be snoring. And then fast asleep.

But he woke up with a hard-on that was well beyond a piss-hard. And he turned toward Hood because the very thought of getting inside of her was the reason he was aroused. But when he felt and then saw that her side of the bed was empty, he was surprised.

Although naked, he got out of bed not

bothering to put on any of his clothes that were strewn all over the room. He instead checked the bathroom, and then made his way downstairs to their gourmet kitchen where he was certain he'd find her. But she wasn't there either. And when she wasn't in the living room, nor the parlor room, nor the music room, he became concerned.

"Hood!" he called out. "Hood!"

But there was no answer in return. He went over to the bay window up front and looked out onto his driveway. He saw the Rolls Royce Boat Tail around the horseshoe driveway, and his Porsche Panamera, but he didn't see her Mercedes convertible. Did she leave without telling him anything? Which would have been okay. But it was almost midnight!

He hurried over to the intercom on the wall and pressed the button. Gate security answered right away. "Yes, sir, Mr. Cassidy?"

"Have you seen my wife?"

"She left, sir, at eleven-eighteen this evening."

She left at eleven at night without waking him up and telling him something? He hurried back upstairs, grabbed his cell phone from off of his night stand, and gave her a call. When it went straight to Voice Mail, as if she had turned it off, he quickly pulled up the GPS of her car's location, an app he had his security chief place on his phone. When he saw where her car was parked, he frowned. "What the fuck is she doing over there?"

Then he hurriedly put on his pants and shoes, threw a pullover shirt over his head, and grabbed his bomber jacket, keys and phone, and hurried out of the room. His heart, for some reason, was hammering.

CHAPTER FOUR

Hood and Ricky sat in her parked Mercedes staring at the dark trailer in front of them. Then Hood, behind the wheel, reached over her brother and pulled out the loaded Glock she kept in her glove compartment.

Ricky was surprised to see her pulling out a gun. "Where you get that from?"

Hood didn't respond. She checked to make certain it was loaded.

"Does Max know you have a gun?"

Hood rolled her eyes. They were always complaining how Max controlled her every movement and how she needed to stop allowing it, but then they loved bringing up Max's name whenever they wanted to control her. She didn't say a word.

But Ricky was still concerned. "Is a gun really necessary, Hood?"

"What you mean is it necessary? You know him like that? You know if he's armed or not?"

"You know I don't know."

"Are you packing?"

"You know I'm not, Hood."

"Then if he is, one of us better be," Hood

said and closed her glove compartment. Then she looked at her big brother. He was a tough guy, but he was more a lover than a fighter. She didn't want him to get in any trouble. "Why don't you stay out here and let me handle it."

But Ricky would hear none of that. He was already taking off his seatbelt. "Don't be stupid," he said to her. "If anybody's staying, it'll be your ass."

"Then nobody's staying," said Hood as she, with her Glock to her side, quickly got out with Ricky, and they made their way across the street to Sonny's trailer.

They'd already decided that Ricky would knock on the door and Hood would stay to the side with her gun at the ready. But what Hood didn't expect was for Ricky to knock so loud a dog from down the street began to howl.

A light came on inside the trailer and without any warning, the trailer door was flown open and Sonny Mathieu was angrily standing at the door. "Your ass better be the Police knocking on my door like that!"

When he saw it was Rita's big brother, he frowned. "What your ass want?"

"May I come in?" Ricky asked him.

"Hell no you ain't coming in my house!"

Hood moved beside her brother with her gun pointed directly at Sonny. "I think he's coming in," she said.

And Ricky easily bogarted his way inside, with Hood right on his tail, both forcing Sonny to back up. Hood slammed the door shut.

"Okay, you're in," said Sonny, looking at that Glock. "Now what do you want?"

Hood was busy looking around the trailer, confident that Ricky could handle that asshole. When she found three bedrooms and nobody in any of them, she returned to the front room. Sonny was still being his obnoxious self.

"I didn't beat your sister," he was claiming. "But you see this gash on the side of my head," he pointed out where Rita had apparently hit him with that lamp. "She's the one who brutalized me!"

"Yeah, right," said Ricky.

"Just what do you want? I told you I didn't touch that bitch."

Hood had to contain her fury. "We just forced our way into your house. Who's the bitch?"

"We wanna know why you thought it was going to be okay for you after you laid a hand on our sister," said Ricky. "Are you stupid, or just dumb?"

"I didn't touch your sister. She's lying like she always does."

"Her injuries aren't lying."

"Man, get out of my face!' His long, straggly hair was whipping. "I didn't touch her. She did that shit to herself."

Ricky and Hood looked at each other. Was this yahoo for real?

"You mean she beat herself up like this?" Ricky asked and punched Sonny on his chin so hard that it knocked him on his ass.

"You mean she beat herself up like this?" Hood asked as she got down on top of Sonny and began pistol whipping him as Ricky was kicking him with his shoe. Then Ricky grabbed him up, flung him across the room, and they both began administering more self-beatings on his ass.

And Sonny was begging. "Okay, I was wrong. I was wrong. Please stop! I didn't mean to hurt her like that! Don't you see you're hurting me? What kind of people are you?"

But Ricky and Hood weren't about to stop to answer his questions. He didn't stop when he was beating Rita's ass, and they were giving back in kind. They were committed to the beatdown and they weren't going halfcocked.

But Hood wasn't going to let it go too far. And when she saw that it was getting close, she had to stop Ricky from crossing the line of a beatdown into a death like she'd experienced before on a retaliation run. But unlike with

JuneBug, Hood was able to pull Ricky back. Because Ricky had a deep sense of right and wrong that stopped him from crossing the line. They had done what they had come there to do, and he was satisfied.

But as Hood was about to put her gun to Sonny's head to warn him against snitching on them, somebody else had apparently entered the house and placed a gun to Hood's head.

Stunned that somebody else was even in the house, she and Ricky both froze. Then Ricky looked at that gun and then looked at the skinny, meth-head-looking white woman holding it.

"Drop it now," the woman said, "or I'm pulling the trigger! And I mean it bitch. I hate y'alls guts! Drop it! You bunch of n-words!"

If the situation wasn't so dire, Hood and Ricky would have bust out laughing. That woman was so scared that she couldn't even bring herself to say the actual word. They were the *n-word* now. But what Hood never understood was why they always had to be a bunch of them? Why not just two n-words, since it was, in fact, just two of them? It was all so ridiculous to Hood!

But that woman wasn't ridiculous. Hood could feel the barrel of that gun pressing against her skull. Conventional wisdom would have been for her to drop her gun and do as the woman said. But Hood could also smell her fear and hear the desperation in that woman's voice. If she dropped that gun, she or Ricky or both of them were dead. Especially as Sonny started throwing up blood.

"Drop it!" the woman screamed again. "Or I'm not gonna stop shooting!"

"I'm dropping it," Hood said as she sat her gun down on the floor. But she knew she couldn't trust that woman to save their lives. And that was what they had to do: save their own lives.

And that was why, as Hood was standing back upright, she pushed the skinny woman away from her, causing the gun to fire wildly. Hood tried to pick up her gun but the woman began firing even as she was knocked down. She was a terrible shot, but it was enough for Ricky to grab Hood and run with her toward the back of the trailer, as the woman was up and running after them, firing even wilder at them.

They both were hoping they would find a back door or a window they could jump out of, or at least find some other getaway. But the woman was running down that hall behind them so fast and firing as if she was some Barney Fyfe so crazily, they knew they were in trouble. The woman had a gun and was scared. That made her even more dangerous than a trained assassin.

Outside, Max had just grabbed his gun out of his Porsche and was making his way to that trailer, too, when he heard shots fired. His heart sank even more than it was already sinking and he ran as fast as he could run, kicking that door open and going inside without hesitation. In the living room, he saw some badly beaten white guy on the floor coughing up blood.

But he didn't say anything to him. He needed to see Hood. He wasn't going to stop until he saw Hood. Even though he still couldn't understand what on earth was she doing there to begin with.

In the back of the house, Hood and Ricky ducked into one of the bedrooms, slammed the door behind them, and hurried to the window. But before they could open the window, the door flung open and the woman was right there with her gun. "Make one more move and y'all dead!" she screamed. "Make one more move!"

They both stopped cold, and held up their hands.

But as soon as they did, they heard another voice. A male's voice. "Drop it!" he yelled.

And both Hood and Ricky knew that voice. They turned around quickly. When they saw that Max was in that house, and that he had a gun pointed at the meth-head, who immediately dropped her weapon, they both sighed relief. Ricky slumped against the wall. Hood slumped against the window frame.

But as Max looked at his wife and brother-in-law, relief didn't describe how he was feeling at all.

Pissed was more his word.

CHAPTER FIVE

The outside of the trailer and the surrounding area was cordoned off. Inside the trailer, Max was leaned against the wall, the sole of one of his shoes pressed against it, too, as he listened to Hood and Ricky give their statements to Police.

And it was exactly as he told them to tell it: That they had been visiting Sonny, a friend, when that crazed, jealous woman broke in and began beating Sonny down with her gun. Then she began firing at Hood and Ricky for being there. They ran, trying to get away from her, when Max showed up. That was the story, and they were telling it.

After Max threatened to finish the job Hood and Ricky started, Sonny, too, corroborated Hood and Ricky's story. And as for the gun the woman claimed Hood had? It was nowhere to be found. Because it was on Max, and no officer of the law anywhere in Illinois, was about to frisk Maxwell Cassidy.

And while they were all being interrogated, and the woman was being arrested, Max made some phone calls so high up that the Superintendent of Police personally ordered the release of Mrs. Cassidy, along with her brother, with no charges to be filed. They were free to go.

But they both could tell, through his silence, just how pissed Max was.

"Drive her car to your house," Max ordered. "She'll pick it up tomorrow."

Ricky wasn't crazy about the way Max was ordering him about, since this wasn't a work situation, but he didn't argue the point. Because he knew those cops would have gladly arrested him and Hood both if Max hadn't shown up. And no telling what Meth Head would have done to them! "Yes, sir," was all he said, and did as he was told.

Max opened the passenger door of his Porsche for Hood. Once she was seated, he walked around and got in under the steering wheel, and then took off without bothering to see if Ricky had left or not. But Ricky was worried about his kid sister more than anything else as they drove away. Sonny was in the hospital and too scared to do anything but go along with their side of the story, which meant they did what they had come there to do. But it could have cost Hood her life. And that didn't sit well with Ricky. And he knew it didn't sit well with Max. Not Max his brother-in-law, and not Max his boss. He might just be out of a job anyway. He drove back to Rita's house.

CHAPTER SIX

The drive to Max's house was so quiet that Hood could only hear the roar of that powerful Porsche engine as they drove. It wasn't until they made it through the gate, got out of the Porsche, and were inside their home did Max say a word. And he lit into Hood.

He tossed his keys on his foyer table and was walking behind her yelling as she made her way into the living room. "A trailer park? Are you out of your fucking mind? I find your ass at a trailer park this time of night, and on that side of town? What's wrong with you, Hood?!"

But Hood wasn't backing down. "He beat the crap out of my sister, Max!"

"I don't care if he beat the crap out of you!" Max flung her around to face him. "You come to me if you have a problem like that. I'll handle it. I'll make sure that asshole pays. But for you to take matters into your own hands like that? Are you kidding me? You're my wife. You're Mrs. Maxwell Cassidy! And Mrs. Maxwell Cassidy does not go on any payback retaliation runs ever! Do you hear me?!"

Max had veins showing in his neck he was so angry. Hood was angry, too, but she knew he wasn't being unreasonable. She understood where he was coming from. But what did he expect her to do? He wouldn't have handled it the way it needed to be handled. He would have relied on the criminal justice system, a system that wasn't about to let that yahoo do time for kicking a black woman's ass. A black woman was so strong, let yahoo tell it, she gave as good as she got. Hood felt her mistake wasn't going on that payback run with Ricky. It was leaving that door unlocked for that meth-head to get inside.

But shots were fired. That scared Hood. For all of her bravado, she was no stone cold anything. Ricky could have gotten hurt. They both could have been killed. She understood what her decision to go could have cost them all.

Max could see her distress because Hood's face showed everything. But he needed her to understand the difference in her lifestyle now. "You are not Hood Riley from the southside of Chicago anymore," he said to her. "You're Mrs. Hood Cassidy now. And I'm telling you right now, Hood, that no wife of mine will be going to beat up her sister's boyfriend. Not ever!"

"I'm sorry I did it, Max," Hood said, "because it turned out to be more dangerous than I thought it was going to be. But I don't understand what you're expecting from me. I'm still me. Just because I married you doesn't change who I am. I don't know how to *not* be me. Somebody beat my sister's ass, I'm beating their ass. That's all I know."

Max exhaled and studied Hood. He knew he was forcing her to become somebody she instinctively wasn't, which wasn't fair. She never promised to change. She only promised to love him.

And that perplexed look on her face was painful for Max to see. "That's all I know," Hood said again. "But now you're telling me I can't be who I am because who I am isn't good enough in your world. That I've got to let you fight my battles. That I've got to lose myself to be with you. What am I supposed to do when you come at me with all of that? Because if that's what you're expecting from me, to become somebody else, then why did you marry me in the first place? So that I wouldn't be who I am?"

"No," said Max. "That's not what I mean."

"That's what you're saying."

Max's temper flared again. "I'm saying common sense should have told your ass not to go to that trailer park!"

"Common sense?" Hood was hot too. "From whose world is this common sense coming from? Because people like me don't wait around for somebody else to fight their battles. They handle that shit themselves. That's all I know, Max, my whole life!"

Tears began to well up in her big, expressive eyes. "And you're right," she said. "I know I'm ghetto. I wish I wasn't so ghetto either, but I am."

Those tears did it for Max. His heart went out to her. But when he touched her arm, she snatched it away from him. "What do you want from me?!" she yelled.

Hood's face was frowned with distress. "My own mama named me Hood. She saw it in me the moment I was born." Hood was rocking side to side, the way she did, Max knew, when she felt cornered. "If I wasn't so ghetto, maybe I wouldn't be so . . . so oddball to everybody. But I don't know what I'm doing yet. We're married but you're never here to show me what you want from me. You've got to give me time to get used to handling it the way it's handled in your world. I've been in my world all my life. I just got in yours."

Max immediately went to Hood, and despite her protestations he pulled her into his arm. "It's alright, baby," he said to her as he could feel her fragility in the bones of her back. "I love who you are. I do. That's why I married you."

Then he pulled her back and looked into her beautiful brownish-green clear eyes, the only person he knew whose eyes only got even clearer when she cried. "All I'm saying is that you can't put yourself at risk. That's all I'm saying. You can't ever put yourself at risk or it'll kill me, Hood. I nearly died when I heard those gunshots. I couldn't get to you fast enough. I give you freedom to do whatever you want to do because I don't like to be caged either. And because I trust you and know you can handle yourself in tough situations. But with that freedom comes a responsibility to yourself, but also to me. And going on retaliation runs isn't responsible, I don't care which world you're coming from! And I say again, my wife is not going to be doing anything remotely similar to that shit you and Ricky pulled tonight. Period. End of discussion."

Hood nodded as he wiped her tears away. "It won't happen again," she said to him.

He stared at her. She was saying the right words, but it was taking all she had to believe it herself. And he wasn't convinced either.

He didn't want to have to do it, but he had no choice. He was going to have to put a clandestine security detail on her at all times.

They would have orders to never approach her unless her life was in danger. And they would report directly to him without telling him her every move unless it involved danger. But her freedom, which he knew she cherished, was going to have to have some limits.

He kissed her on her forehead and pulled her into his arms. He never liked security on himself, and he'd always said it would take a drastic change in situation for him to put security on her. But gunshots fired in some fucking trailer, and his wife in the middle of a gun battle? That, for him, qualified as drastic.

CHAPTER SEVEN

An hour later and a Lincoln Aviator SUV was parked on a dead-end street. A Mustang drove up behind it, Toby Fitch got out of the Mustang and walked up to the SUV, and then he got in on the backseat. Breena Novak, decked down in a fur coat, was seated on that backseat. "What happened?"

"You were right. She showed up with her brother. They both beat Sonny's ass just like you said they would."

"And Pam?"

"She showed up before it got out of hand. But shots were fired."

Breena looked at Toby. "On our end?"

Toby nodded. "She had no choice, Bree. They were trying to take her out. The girl, Hood, brought a gun with her to the beat down. Pam fired shots alright, but she was careful not to hit either one of them."

Breena exhaled. "Good. That would have been premature."

"Very," said Toby.

"What about the cops? They showed up too?"

"Oh yeah. In force. But guess who came

before the cops got there?"

"Who?"

"Maxwell Cassidy himself."

Breena was shocked. "Max showed up?"

"He showed up, Bree. I was shocked too. That bastard actually showed up himself. Not his lawyers. Not his mini-me Jason Bogart. *He* showed up. And you know what that means."

"He actually loves that hood rat," said Breena, with sadness in her eyes.

Toby nodded his agreement. "Why else would he bother? His ass never showed up when Camille was in trouble. He had the lawyers handle it after she got arrested for her umpteenth DUI, or whatever jam she was in. But he never once showed up himself. He has to really love that girl."

Breena exhaled. All she needed. "What did he do?"

"He made some phone calls apparently because the cops didn't even press charges against their asses. Hood Rat Riley and her brother were able to walk away scot-free."

"So he's got the Police in his pocket?"

"Deep in his pocket," said Toby.

"Okay. At least we know what we're dealing with now. Good trial run."

"What about Pam? Bail her out?"

"And blow our cover this early? Hell no,"

said Breena. "Get word to her that she's to stay put until it's done."

"And when will that be?"

"When we close that Albright deal in New York. That's when Max will lay eyes on me again for the first time in a decade. That'll at least be the beginning of the end."

"And what is the end, Bree?" Toby asked her. "You'll be in the same room with Max again for the first time in a decade. And we both know you still love him. What is the end going to look like if you let your heart get in the way?"

But Breena gave him a cold look. "Stay in your lane, Toby Fitch. That ain't your business. Stay in your lane."

Then the back door was opened by the driver of the SUV, which Toby knew meant it was time for him to leave. He got out, the driver got back into the SUV, and the SUV drove off.

Toby watched it leave. But he was still wondering why in the world was he still hooked up with crazy? That man wasn't just Max Cassidy anymore. He was Max Cassidy, the billionaire. They were fucking around with a billionaire's wife. A billionaire with the Chicago PD in his pocket! *Were they insane*?

But there was no turning back now. He made his bed and he had to lie in it.

He got in his Mustang, and sped away

too.

CHAPTER EIGHT

The next morning, after that tongue-lashing Max had put on her, Hood, in one of his big shirts, was walking up the west staircase carrying a tray filled with a hot breakfast planned by, cooked by, and serviced by Hood. She'd never done anything like it in her entire life. She never had to cook for anybody but herself. But she was determined to be the best wife she could be. Rita could talk all day long about not showing him how she truly felt about him or he'd exploit it. She could declare Max had too much power over her. But she loved him. And was going to make her marriage worked. Max brought a lot to the table. She had to bring what she could. And she knew it couldn't just be her body or that would get old to him real quick. It had to be all of her. She had to give him all she had to give.

Max was still in bed, lying on his back and fielding messages on his phone, when she walked into their bedroom. He didn't bother to look away from a urgent text he was reading, and Hood did feel a bit of hesitation that he might not like being disturbed early in the morning. But his breakfast was hot and ready.

She'd slaved over that stove to get it as good as she could get it. She wasn't turning around.

"Good morning," she said to him with a smile on her face as she stood there with that gold-encrusted serving tray in her hand.

But Max held up a *just a sec* finger as he text a response to that urgent message.

Hood didn't like it. A part of her wanted to cuss his ass out for not even glancing her way. She knew he was a busy man. She knew he ran an empire. But he couldn't even take a second to say good morning to her, or to acknowledge her presence even if he didn't acknowledge her hard work preparing breakfast in bed for him? It didn't take Rita to tell her that his inattention to her sometimes was just plain wrong.

"I said good morning, Max," Hood said to him. "Put that phone down for two seconds and at least say something to me!"

Max frowned a frown of cold anger and was ready to unleash it without reservation. Nobody spoke to him that way! But as soon as he looked away from his phone and saw Hood standing there, with that pure, ultra-sincere look on her beautiful face, he softened. Nobody did that to him but her. And when he saw that tray filled with a hot breakfast she was carrying, presumably just for him, he felt as if he'd almost blown it. "For me?" he asked her.

Hood saw that anger he was about to unleash, and it bothered her, but she managed to nod her head. "All for you," she said.

"Well now," Max said as he sat his phone on the night stand and sat up in bed. He still had urgent business to handle, but it was going to have to wait.

Hood sat the tray across his lap, said a prayer of thanks with him, and then laid across the bed at his feet and watched him eat.

"Oh it's good, Hood," he said as he bit into a toast and then into a hash brown.

"Is it?" Hood was hopeful.

"Very good. I didn't know your ass could cook like this. I mean, I know it can cook. But I didn't know it could cook *food* like this."

Hood laughed. "I try," she said.

"Oh you did more than that. It's delicious." And it was to Max. Either that or he was very hungry. "You aren't going to join me?"

"Nope," Hood said. "I got full just looking at all that food. Now I don't want any of it."

Max looked at Hood as he ate. She was never a big girl, but he didn't want her skinny either and she'd been losing weight. "Here, eat this," he said, placing a slice of bacon to her mouth.

She bit a piece.

"Eat the whole thing," he said to her.

"I'm not hungry."

"That's not the point. Eat it."

Hood rolled her eyes, but she took the bacon from Max's hand and ate it all. "Satisfied?" she asked him.

"Better," he said as he was still chomping down. Hood began heading for the bathroom.

"Where are you going?"

"To take a shower," said Hood as she walked into the bathroom and closed the door behind her.

And once she was in the shower, her face leaned back as the warm water careened all over her naked body. And she thought about last night and that big argument she and Max had had. Because it was all about who she was as a person and if she could change her very nature to conform to Max's world. She knew she had to make some changes to be with a man like him, but she always thought they would be about how she interacted at social functions with him, or how she managed his household. She never thought the changes would be internal. She never thought Max expected her to change her entire world view, and all of her own defense mechanisms, just because she became his wife. When she didn't ask nor expect him to change anything for her.

She knew their marriage would be unequal and that Max, given his power, his position, the fact that he was older than her, would be the boss in their union in every way. And forget not being in his league. They weren't even in the same ball park! And Hood knew, if she didn't stand up for herself, she'd never get on the same field with a man like Max. He wouldn't respect her in the end. She knew Rita was right about that part. And that was unsettling to Hood. It felt as if she would have to get her whole body through the eye of a needle to be able to ever fully please Max.

But if that was what it took, she just wasn't going to please him.

But that kind of thinking, she also knew, didn't help a damn thing. She kept bathing and decided to stop overthinking it. Things would work out eventually, she believed, because they had to. Because Max was the best thing that ever happened to her and she wasn't losing him. Even if it meant making more changes than she thought was reasonable. Maybe she had to do some body contortions. Whatever it was, she had to find that balance. She had to find that sweet spot.

But as she continued to bathe, she heard the bathroom door opening and then she saw Max walk over to the toilet and, without lifting the lid, peeing. Which meant he had finished his breakfast. Would probably go back to bed, given how tired he was last night.

But Max saw the outline of Hood's naked body through the shower glass and the piss hard he was releasing became a full-blown hard-on and there was no way he was going anywhere else, or waiting another second longer, without getting inside of her again.

After wiggling out the last of his pee, he made his way to the shower stall. Hood could see him coming across his large bathroom's marbled floor, and she could also see that he was coming already completely aroused. Which only aroused her. Which caused her to go from thinking about something as major as their marriage, to something completely different.

As soon as Max stepped into the shower and closed the door, he had only to turn her toward him before their lips locked into a kiss so passionate that Hood had to pull back from him in order to breathe.

But once she got one good breath in, he was on her lips again. And then he was kissing her neck and her chest and when he got to her breasts and began to suck, she knew then it was going to be wonderful. As wonderful as it was in that limo. Now she wanted him as desperately as he wanted her.

But Max was beyond desperation. He had to get inside of her in the worst way. That was why he lifted her into his arms, wrapped her legs around him, and then leaned her against the shower wall. And when he entered her, and she felt the fullness of his entry, she started moaning as loudly as Max was groaning. And Max was loud!

As soon as he entered her and felt the tightness that always defined the way Hood felt whenever he was inside of her, he lost all control. He had her against the wet, slick wall and started pumping his ass off.

Hood had her arms around his neck and was bouncing in his arms because of how hard he was going at it, and when he started kissing her again as he did her, she closed her eyes and could hardly believe how great it felt.

Max felt it too as he kissed her and fucked her and couldn't seem to even attempt to find that slow rhythm he was usually able to produce. It felt too intense to slow down. He, instead, started speeding up.

Hood didn't think it could get any more real until Max began to bang even harder. He was going so hard that her ass was slapping against that shower wall and she was loving every second of it.

For minutes on end all that could be

heard were their moans and groans and the sound of slapping flesh that drowned out even the sound of the running water. Max couldn't get enough of Hood. It was what he craved whenever he was away from her. And despite all those gorgeous ladies that were constantly in his face, trying to seduce their way into his bed, and some even getting his attention, it was always Hood he wanted above all else. It was always this old-soul of a girl who was all about doing the right thing, and all about truth and being for real. Who was all heart. And she had to be, Max knew, to have won over his cold heart.

And all of those emotions he felt for her became encapsulated into feelings so deep and so intense that when they came it was a thunderous cum. Neither one of them could contain the joy they felt and the unbridled feelings of love that tore through their bodies as they came. Max was still pumping harder and harder, banging his ass off, and Hood was groaning louder and louder as they came. So loud that when her orgasm was at its apex, she couldn't bear it and was trying to break free from him.

But Max wasn't about to let her go. He held onto her and pumped into her with even more roughness. And when his own climax was at its apex he started pouring into her as if a levee had broken, and he was grunting so hard that he didn't think he could bear it either. But he did. Both of them did. Until they were so well-spent that Max finally stopped putting it on her and they fell against that shower wall holding each other up.

They remained where they were for several seconds longer as they both were attempting to get their erratic breathing back under control and Max was still forcing out the last of his enormous load. And then they finally looked into each other's still lust-filled eyes. And all they saw in each other's eyes was love. And Max kissed her again. And then he was staring at her again.

"I expected you to eat and go back to bed. Why are you up so early?" she asked him.

Max smiled. "Your ass," he said, which caused Hood to smile too.

But after they showered to clean themselves up and Max was getting out of the stall ahead of Hood, he added another reason. "I've got to fly to New York to take care of some business," he said as if it was no big deal.

Hood, at first, thought he was joking. But when he didn't glance back at her with that smile she loved, but he grabbed a towel and headed for their bedroom, she turned off the water and got out too. After grabbing a towel to dry off herself, she walked into the bedroom.

Max, already dried off and with the towel around his waist, was in their room-sized closet grabbing a brand-new pair of briefs and a brand-new t-shirt from out of one of the drawers of the massive center island, and tearing open their packaging.

Hood had stopped drying off and held the towel up against her body as she watched him. "But you just got back in town yesterday," she said.

"And I've got to go again," Max said.

"But. . ." Hood was so disappointed that she didn't know how to express it. She wasn't accustomed to giving another human being so much control over her emotions that they could disappoint her so easily. And it was beginning to alarm her. "When are you leaving?" she asked him.

"After I go check on a couple of construction sites," he said as he put on his underwear. "I'll be flying out after that."

"But what about the dinner party tonight? I thought you said we had to attend it in order for you to get the mayor on board with your proposal."

"And we will attend it. I should be back this afternoon at the latest. The deal is closed.

I'm only there to sign the contract that would put an influx of Cassbars into the Czech Republic. It's a done deal."

"But what if your negotiators didn't close the deal?" Hood asked.

Max didn't even want to think about any delays that significant. "It's a done deal," he said again as he put on his t-shirt. Then he looked at Hood. He could see her disappointment. "I'll be back in time for that dinner party, Hood. Stop worrying. I won't leave you on the hook like that. Okay?"

Hood didn't give a flip nickel about that dinner party. It was their marriage she was concerned about. And she needed to hear far more from him than what she was hearing. He was acting as if he was still a bachelor who didn't have to work at all on their marriage the way she was working on it. And Hood wasn't having it.

And because her expressive face hid nothing, Max could see his answer was not satisfying her at all. "What is it?" he asked her.

"This won't work, Max."

Max's heart dropped. Was she tired of him already? "What won't work?"

"This! You gone all the time. This can't work."

"I have an empire to run, Hood. You

know that."

"Then you better figure out a way for me to be a part of that empire because I'm not sitting at home waiting for you to drop by every now and then and we call this a marriage. I'm not the one, Max. I am not the one."

She had that look of sincerity Max loved, except when she was using it to tell him about himself. But it wasn't as if she was wrong. "Okay," he said. "Point taken. When I get back this time, we'll sit down and work something out."

He didn't offer for her to go with him *this time*. He never offered. And she wasn't going to beg. But she was going to hold him to his word. "You promise?" she asked in a way so innocent that it touched Max's heart. She had the purest heart of any human being he'd ever met.

He went to her and pulled her into his arms, causing her towel to drop because of the suddenness of his embrace. "I promise," he said to her as he held her. "We were in Europe for a month and that backed up a lot of my stateside decisions that can only be made at my level only. So I'm making up for lost time now. But I promise you it won't be like this always. And once I get back, we'll come up with a game plan that will include you too."

Hood looked at him. He placed his hands on the sides of her face. "Does that meet with your approval, Mrs. Cassidy?" he asked her.

Hood smiled. "I think I can live with that," she said, and Max laughed.

But when the laughter slowly began to recede, and as Max could feel her nakedness against his own near-nakedness, he knew he was trapped again. No woman alive had ever turned him on as easily as Hood was able to do. Sometimes all it took was a look of her big, vivid eyes, or something as simple as the way she sipped her wine. And he rarely could have her naked around him and do nothing. And this time was no exception.

Max lifted her up, carried her to their bed, opened her wide, and began eating her in such a momentous way that it worked them both up again. And within minutes he had dropped his draws, climbed on top of her, and was inside of her once again.

CHAPTER NINE

It took Hood and Ricky both to slide that big screen TV into Ricky's Jeep. And Ricky smiled. "I told you it would fit!"

"It barely fits, Ricky."

"When is barely a problem? Barely means it fits. That's the issue. It's in there."

"This big-ass TV."

"That's right. And a steal for the price I paid for it. And I don't have TV the first in my house. I need one."

Then Ricky looked at Hood. "Think I'm weird not having a TV?"

"What's weird?"

Ricky laughed. "I forgot who I was asking," he said, and Hood laughed too.

"I just didn't need one," said Ricky. "I was spending most of my time with the ladies. I was never home. But now that I'm back on the market again."

"Now that yet another lady has kicked you out."

"That too," said Ricky. "But now that I'm back up for grabs, I figure I need some company in the meantime."

Hood understood that. They were in Shandlet, a suburb just outside of Chicago, and she had agreed to help him. She just never imagined it would be heavy lifting help. "Let's just get this thing to your house," she said.

Ricky grinned. "Don't tell me you're worried about what Max will say if he knew his wife was hanging out at the Walmart with her big brother."

"Boy bye! You trippin'. Max is not like that and you know it. He doesn't care if I go to Walmart. There was a time, not that long ago, when I couldn't even afford Walmart. I was getting everything from secondhand stores. Walmart was above my paygrade then," she added as she got in on the front passenger seat.

"I hear you," Ricky said as he got in behind the steering wheel. "I been there too." And although he was all laughs as he began driving off, he wasn't entirely joking. He glanced over at Hood. "But for real," he said, "things okay on the home front?"

Hood knew Max was super-private and didn't like her discussing anything that went on in their household, but it wasn't just him involved. She was involved too. And if she couldn't talk to her siblings about it, who was she going to talk to? She'd always been the odd-girl-out who was never good at making friends. Ricky and Rita were her friends. "It's okay," she said.

"He was so pissed last night," said Ricky, "I thought he was gonna beat your ass right in front of those cops."

Hood looked at Ricky as if he had grown an extra pair of eyes. "Beat my ass? Who? Nobody's beating my ass, okay?"

"But he was really upset with you. For real though, Hood. And I don't understand what he expected you to do. Your sister got her ass whipped and he didn't think we were going to do something about that?"

"He's not from our world, Ricky. He believes I should have let him handle it."

"Yeah, right. We know what kind of handling a guy like him would have done. He would have brought them to justice. A white man beat a black woman and justice will be served? Give me a break!"

Hood knew Max was more gangster than Ricky realized, but that was Max's business.

"Where is he now anyway? At the office?"

"He's doing some site visits and then he's going to New York."

Ricky looked at her. "Are you serious? But he just got back in town!"

"He has an empire to maintain," Hood said, echoing what Max had said to her.

But Ricky was shaking his head. "Ain't that much empire-maintaining in this world when he has a brand-new bride he needs to pay attention to. You let him get away with too much, Hood. For real. Rita's right about that. That's not good."

"I don't let him get away with shit, alright? He's a grown-ass man. I don't tell him what he can and cannot do."

"But he tells you."

"You don't know what you're talking about. Max doesn't--"

But then suddenly the Jeep was bumped from behind, causing both of them to jerk forward.

"What the fuck?" Ricky said as he looked through his side mirror ready to cuss somebody out. That was when he saw a white Chevy Blazer SUV riding his bumper.

Hood looked out of her side mirror too. "Who are they?"

"I was gonna ask you that same question."

"Couple white boys all I see. I don't know them."

"I don't know them either," said Ricky. "Which meant that shit was intentional."

And as if to prove that it was, the Blazer bumped the Jeep again, causing them to jerk again.

"Ah shit," said Ricky. "And you're in the car too? Max Cassidy's wife? Oh hell no!"

Ricky hit the gas pedal with such force that Hood jerked backwards as he sped away from the SUV behind them.

"What do I have to do with it?" Hood was asking as they fled. "You think they're after me?"

"Why else would two white boys be ramming my Jeep on purpose? I been keeping my nose clean since I came to this town."

"Your nose wasn't so clean last night. Maybe they're friends of Sonny's."

"He ain't got no friends," said Ricky as he turned a corner on nearly two wheels and kept on going. His aim was to get off of those backroads he liked to travel, but that Chevy Blazer stayed on his tail. Which only further proved his point.

The security detail that was ordered to remain away from Hood just enough to stay in the shadows, but not enough to be useless if she needed them, suddenly began speeding behind the two speeding vehicles. They were fighting to make up ground and ride the Blazer's bumper, to spin them out and off the trail of the

Jeep, but the Blazer and the Jeep had a small head start that they couldn't surmount. But they kept trying.

"They're still behind us," said Hood as she kept looking through the rear view. "They're still behind us, Ricky. I'm gonna call 911," she added, as she began pulling out her cell phone.

But before she could press the emergency button on her phone, the Blazer bumped them again with such force that Ricky began swerving and almost lost control, and Hood's cell phone flew to the floor.

"Ricky, be careful!" Hood yelled as he wrestled with the wheel.

"I'm trying!" Ricky yelled back. "I'm trying!"

And he kept trying even as they were bumped again, which could have caused him to lose all control. But he didn't. And as soon as he straightened back up, he floored it again and kept on flying.

Until he turned down another side road that would lead them to a major thoroughfare. They were making progress despite the setbacks. But before they could make it to civilization again, they heard the sirens.

They both looked through the side mirrors and saw that the Chevy Blazer had turned on police sirens that were on its dashboard and the driver was on the blowhorn finally identifying himself as a cop and ordering them to stop at once.

The security detail, that had made up most of the ground, eased back when they heard the sirens.

Ricky and Hood were puzzled too. "They're cops?" asked Ricky, floored.

"Don't stop, Ricky! It could be a setup," said Hood, although she was equally confused.

"Yeah it could be," said Ricky. "Just get 911 on the phone.

Hood grabbed for her phone from off the floor and called 911. As soon as the operator came on, she told her what was going on. But she was clear. "Let them know we're going to stop," she said over the phone, "but not on this backroad. We're going where other people can see us. They didn't say who they were, they don't have any police anything on that SUV they're driving, there's no way we're stopping on this backroad. And because we don't know who they really are, I don't know if we should stop at all."

"If they have sirens on, you have to stop ma'am," said the 911 operator. "We do have unmarked cars, ma'am."

But Hood wasn't trying to hear that. "Keep going, Ricky. Don't stop until we get around other people. We have that right. They didn't identify themselves when they were bumping us like fools. Keep going," Hood ordered.

But Ricky was already of that same mind. "Don't worry," he said. "I'm not about to stop on this backstreet after what they did to us."

And he didn't. He kept on driving, and Hood kept the 911 operator on the phone, until they were on the main road and Ricky pulled into a Best Buy parking lot and came to a stop. Hood kept them on the phone even after that.

But if they thought the cops were going to behave any way other that angry and aggressive, they had another thought coming.

Both plainclothes detectives had their guns drawn and pointed downward as they hurried toward the Jeep. They were ordering Ricky and Hood to get out as they hurried.

"Tell them who you are as soon as we get out, Hood," Ricky urged anxiously. "Drop Max's name. Make it clear you're his wife. Drop the hell out of Max's name, you hear me?"

"Yes, Ricky, I got it," said Hood, terrified too. She didn't like cops any more than he did!

Ricky pressed down the window. "May I help you, Officer?" he said as soon as they walked up.

"Get out of the car!" the Officer

screamed. "And get out now with your hands in the air!"

Hood frowned. "For what?" she asked. "Y'all didn't say who y'all were!"

"Get out!" the other officer, on the passenger side, yelled at Hood.

Hood hated doing it, but she knew she had to. "I'm Maxwell Cassidy's wife and I want to know what we did wrong?" she said, to Ricky's relief.

But if they thought Max's name would save the day with a couple of hellbent cops like the two they were encountering, they were sadly mistaken.

As soon as they stepped out of their vehicle, each cop took one sibling and threw them to the ground. And once the cop had Ricky on the ground, he pressed his shoe against Ricky's face.

"What are you doing to my brother?" Hood yelled anxiously. "Leave my brother alone!"

Ricky was in severe pain, but he wasn't about to let those cops see it.

"What did we do?" Hood was yelling. "What did we do?!"

"You know what you did. You fled an officer's command," one of the cops yelled at her.

"You didn't command shit from us!" Hood yelled. "You didn't tell us who you were. You just started bumping our Jeep!"

"And you stole that TV," the other cop added.

Hood, stunned, tried to look at that cop as he was cuffing her. "We *what*?"

"Hood, let it go," Ricky said to his sister. He'd had far more encounters with the cops than she'd ever had. He knew what they were capable of. "Just let it go!"

And Hood did as Ricky told her to do. Because she knew now, like he knew, that they were fighting a losing battle. They were two powerless people and those cops knew it. It was going to take nothing short of Max, *again*, to get them out of this crazy situation. And that, to Hood, was nothing short of a shame.

CHAPTER TEN

Max drove his Porsche onto his newest development site in Wheaton and stopped in front of the makeshift office. As he got out and looked around, he was pleased with the progress. On budget and ahead of schedule? He couldn't ask for anything more. He went into the makeshift office near the front gate.

The site's general manager, Ned Barkley, was just getting off of the phone when Max walked in. He got on his feet and extended his hand. "Hey, Chief, how you doing? I thought you were still in Arizona."

"Got back yesterday," Max said as they shook hands. "Looking better out there than it did before I left."

Barkley nodded. "It's coming along. We're making some real good progress."

Max stared at him. "But? There's always

a but with your ass."

Barkley smiled. "You don't even realize what you just said, do you, Boss? But and ass? As in *butt* and ass?"

But Max didn't crack a smile. "I have all day for this bullshit?"

Barkley remembered who he was dealing with. The Ice Man. Coldest motherfucker on record, as he used to joke. "There is a but," he admitted.

Max waited for him to say more, but he was hesitating. "I don't have all day, Bark."

"Rita Riley," Barkley suddenly said.

Max had not expected to hear that name. "What about her? I heard she's a hard worker."

"Oh, she's a very hard worker. In a *slave driver* kind of hard worker."

"What's that supposed to mean?"

"We need an experienced project manager, Max."

"You're her supervisor. She's a trainee. You're supposed to be teaching her."

"And I am! But she won't listen. She's alienating every contractor I hire. Half of them are threatening to walk off the job if she don't let up." He exhaled. "Look, I know she's your wife's sister ---"

Max was immediately offended. "Don't give me that bullshit! Either she's up to the job or she's not. Nothing else matters."

And Barkley knew it was true. When it came to his business, Max didn't fuck around. Everybody knew that. "I try to tell her to ease up. That the work will get done. And she'll nod and say okay and then go right back to cracking the whip. These are proud men, Max. They'll walk off the job, I'm telling you they will."

Max exhaled, and then he nodded. "Get her in here."

Barkley grabbed the Walkie Talkie. "Rita Riley, come to the office," he said into the speaker. "Rita Riley, get to the office!" And then he sat the Walkie Talkie back on the desk.

Max opened his suit coat, placed his hands in his pockets, and walked over to the window to look further at the progress. Barkley exhaled again. Like most men who worked for Max, he couldn't stand him either. Arrogant to his core, was how he saw him. Rich his whole life. Never knew what struggling was. A Richie Rich prick! One day somebody was going to put that bastard in his place, and he was going to enjoy watching the carnage.

And then Rita walked into the office.

Max turned and looked at her. She was dressed in jeans, a tucked-in blouse and a blazer, and she had enough sawdust on her coat to let Max know she wasn't just barking out orders but was doing the work too. Her face was still badly bruised from what that asshole did to her, and even with those shades she was wearing, it was obvious she had taken a serious beatdown. But she still showed up for work. That was what he liked about her. Like Hood, she took things seriously and didn't play when it came to getting jobs done. But also like Hood, she could be as stubborn as the day was long.

"Oh hey Max," Rita said when she entered the office. "I didn't expect to see you here."

"How's it going?"

"Alright. At least I thought it was. What's up?" She looked from Max to Barkley, and then back to Max.

And Max didn't mince words. He never had time to. "You're having a problem with the crew," he said.

In a way, Rita knew that was going to be the issue. But she wasn't going to let Barkley or anybody else claim that it was the real issue. "Ain't no problem," she said. "They just wanna work when they feel like working and I'm not having it."

"That's not the case," said Barkley.

"That is the case!" Rita shot back. "When they decide to work they work well, but then they wanna sit on their asses half the time and do nothing. And they wanna get an attitude with me because I remind them that they aren't on their clock when they're on this job site. They're on Cassidy Incorporated's clock when they're on this site, and while they're on the Cassidy clock they had better produce. That's how we got as much done as we got done. Barkley claims I'm cracking the whip, but that's what I thought you hired me to do," she said to Max. "Half of this work wouldn't be done if I wasn't cracking it. He sure as hell isn't cracking it."

Max knew instinctively that Rita was telling the truth because none of the Riley siblings were liars. In his assessment of them, they were all honorable people with an old-fashioned sense of integrity you could take to the bank. They were all hard workers, and expected the same from those around them. That was why Max was willing to give them a chance in his organization. That was why Max was nodding his head now and agreeing with Rita. "Keep cracking that whip," he said to her.

Although Barkley didn't like it, Rita felt a swell of satisfaction. "Thank you, sir."

"And if they don't like it," Max added, "tell them to take it up with me."

Rita smiled as she nodded. Finally somebody was hearing her! "Yes, sir," she said and glanced at Barkley.

He absolutely didn't like it, but that was between him and Max now. Which meant it wasn't between anybody because Max's word was final.

"Anything else?" Max asked Barkley.

"No, sir," said Barkley. "But what am I supposed to do if they walk off the job?"

Max frowned even as his cell phone started ringing. "You fire their asses and hire a new crew. What are you asking me a question like that for? I'm not going to be hostage to the people I'm paying good money to work for me, are you out of your fucking mind? You fired their asses, that's what you do!"

When Max looked at the Caller ID on his phone and saw that it was Dale Perry, his security chief, he answered. "Yeah?"

"I just got a call from Mrs. Cassidy's security detail."

Max had ordered Dale to place a clandestine security detail on Hood wherever she went, but they were ordered to remain in the shadows and never reveal themselves to her unless she was in some sort of danger. Just hearing that there was a problem caused Max's heart to squeeze. Dale wouldn't be calling him if it was minor. "And?" he asked Dale.

"And the cops just arrested her, sir."

Max stopped in his tracks. "Arrested

her?" Max was floored. "They arrested *my* wife?"

When Rita heard that her sister had been arrested, she was floored too. "They arrested Hood?" she asked Max.

"What are they claiming she did?" Max asked Dale.

"She supposedly stole a TV is the nearest we can figure."

"A *TV*?" Max could hardly believe it. "Where is she?"

"Shandlet PD. I've got lawyers headed there now."

"Fuck the lawyers!" Max said angrily as he began running out of that office. But Rita began running right behind him.

"Where are you going?" Barkley yelled at Rita. "I'm not giving you permission to leave this site!"

But Rita wasn't thinking about that man. When it came to her sister, nobody had to give her shit. She was taking permission! Just as she hopped into Max's Porsche without permission too. Hood was in trouble. It went without saying she was going to see about her baby sister.

It went without saying to Max, too, as he ordered her to buckle up as he sped away.

CHAPTER ELEVEN

The Porsche came to a rolling stop in front of the police station and Max and Rita jumped out and ran inside. Rita was convinced that there was no way forty-year-old Max was going to outrun her, but he easily did. He flung open that door and was inside of that building by the time Rita made it to the top of the steps. But she was right behind him.

Max expected some pushback at the front desk where the most obnoxious people seemed to always be working, but there was no need for any front desk intervention. The police chief, who had discovered exactly who they had behind bars, was waiting for him.

"Mr. Cassidy, hello," he said, extending his hand. "I'm the chief of police here in Shandlet and--"

"Where's my wife?" Max asked him urgently, as he refused to shake the hand of anybody that would arrest his wife on what he knew was bullshit.

"We didn't realize she was your wife, sir, until after--"

"Where is she?!" Max asked angrily. "Does it look like I want to hear a fucking story from you? Where's my wife?"

The chief swallowed hard. He wanted to rip those detectives apart himself when he found out who they had processed in. "Right this way, sir," he said and began escorting Max and Rita down a long, narrow hall.

Chief of Police was on the door that he opened. It was his office. And not only was Hood sitting in a chair against the wall in that office, but to Max and Rita's surprise, Ricky was sitting in there too. And one side of his face was bruised.

Rita expected Max to run to Hood and comfort her. But Max always had that cool exterior whenever he was in public. She could tell everything inside of him wanted to run to Hood, but he didn't blow his cover. He kept his cool. He looked at his wife and brother-in-law and kept it together.

"They've been released I take it," Max said to the chief.

"I wanted to release them right away, sir," said the chief. "But because they were already processed through before I discovered who they were, it's no longer up to me. Only the state attorney can give permission to drop the charges once they've been entered in the system."

"Then where is he? Get his ass over here so we can get this over with."

"It's a she, sir, and she's on the way. I've already phoned and explained the situation to her."

Max exhaled. Life would be fine if it wasn't for the people! "Give us some privacy until she gets here," he said to the chief.

Ricky looked at the chief. He was all cooperation now, but he was just as nasty as his officers before Max arrived. But he didn't mix it up with Max. He allowed Max to kick him out of his own office. The chief left.

Hood was sitting there, her legs folded and flapping as if she was more impatient than worried. She just wanted to go home.

But Max still didn't go to her. He began to pace around the room. Rita, disappointed that he always had to keep his guard up in public, went to her sister and brother. "You guys okay?" she asked them.

"We're okay," Ricky said.

Rita grabbed his face. "They did this to you?"

"Not like you think. It happened when they threw me on the ground to cuff me."

Rita was confused. "But what did they arrest you for?"

"I bought a flat screen TV at Walmart and Hood was helping me get it in my Jeep. Then all of a sudden we're driving and minding our own business and this SUV bumps us and chases us. Then they decide to turn on their sirens and arrest us for stealing a TV I clearly bought, and for resisting arrest and evading an officer when we did no such thing. Just trumped-up bullshit."

"What about you, Hood?" asked Rita. "Did they hurt you too?"

Max continued pacing, but he looked over at Hood when Rita asked her that question.

Hood shook her head. "No. I'm okay. I just wanna get out of here."

"You will. Max's lawyers are on the way."

But as it turned out, there was no need for lawyers. Because as soon as the chief returned with the state attorney, Max pulled her aside and they had a serious conversation. Although Max was playing it cool with them, his voice was animated as he spoke to that attorney. Then she asked Hood and Ricky a couple of questions that seemed more for appearances sake than anything else, and then she ordered their release. As simple as that.

But it wasn't as simple as that for Hood and Max. Hood wanted to kick their asses. Max wanted to know why those cops didn't ask to see the receipt and instead believed what some Karen told them. "I want them fired," Max said to the chief.

Hood would normally refuse to go along with anybody losing their livelihood for something that wasn't that deep. But it was that deep because if she hadn't been the wife of who she was the wife of, she and Ricky would still be in that jail and could possibly go on trial for something they didn't do. It was deep.

"Don't worry, sir," the chief proclaimed. "They won't be working in this jurisdiction ever again."

"Oh they won't be working as cops in any jurisdiction ever again," said Max. "I'll see to that." And Max wasn't whistling Dixie either.

They left the building, with Rita riding with Ricky in his processed-out Jeep, while Hood rode with Max to the airfield.

But as they drove off, Toby Fitch had driven his Mustang behind a Chinese restaurant and was parking beside that same Chevy Blazer that had stopped Hood and Ricky. And those same too detectives were sitting inside.

Toby pressed down the window. "You're dealing with Maxwell Cassidy," he said to them. "Expect to be fired."

"That was a part of the deal," said the driver of the Blazer. "That's why the pay had to be retirement-type money."

"It is," said Toby as he handed him two envelopes.

The driver handed one to the other detective in the Blazer and they both looked inside.

"All cash," said Toby. "No Uncle Sam, no tracers."

The cops smiled.

"Is it as agreed?" asked Toby.

"Oh yeah," said the driver. "Exactly as agreed."

"Alright gentlemen. You don't know me, and I don't know you."

"But I don't get it. Those two are getting off probably as we're speaking right now. They won't face any charges. What's this about, if I can ask?"

"No," said Toby.

The driver was confused. "No? No what?"

"You can't ask," said Toby. "Enjoy your retirement, gentlemen," he added, and then drove away.

CHAPTER TWELVE

Whenever Max was upset with her, Hood was beginning to notice, he became cool as a cucumber, as if he had to have time to process what he was going to say to her. That was why he said nothing to her at the police station. That was why no words were spoken as he drove them to the airfield. But once they arrived and they saw that his private plane was ready for takeoff, Max put his Porsche in park and turned toward Hood, who sat on his passenger seat. "No more of that Batman and Robin shit with Ricky," he said to her. "Stay away from Ricky."

But Hood wasn't going to let her brother take the fall for something he didn't do. "Why would I have to stay away from my own brother? He didn't do anything wrong."

"That's not the point."

"Then what is the point? Because he's a black man who the cops can arrest for no reason?"

"Yes!" Max said emphatically. "That's exactly why. Your bad temper and cops don't mix. You'll end up getting yourself and your brother killed if they come at you the wrong way." Then he frowned. "It'll kill me if something happens to you, Hood. Especially if I'm not here to get you out of that situation."

"I can take care of myself, Max."

"Did you take care of yourself when they arrested you? Did you take care of yourself in that trailer?"

Hood looked out of the window. "No," she admitted.

Max turned her head back toward him. He smoothed down a strand of her soft hair. And then they leaned forward and their foreheads met. "I don't want you to go, Max," Hood said.

If he wasn't going to be working twenty-four-seven when he did get to New York, he would take her with him. But that would be as impractical as it was unnecessary. "I'll be back this afternoon," he said. "I'll be back in more than enough time to make it to the dinner party, and to have our discussion about your role in the company."

"You have to be back in time. I've never been to a party like that and I don't know how it all works. You have to be back in time, Max."

Max smiled. Although Hood was as tough as any woman he'd ever met, she was also so innocent that it sometimes shocked him. He kissed her. "I'll be back in time," he reassured her when their lips parted. "No need to be afraid."

Hood was offended. "Me? Afraid to go to some party? Please!"

Max laughed. "Didn't mean to step on your toes."

Hood smiled too. "Just get your ass back here."

"Will do, Boss," said Max, saluting.

But then his look became serious again. "I know you've only just reunited with your siblings and you love being around them, but I need you to start thinking about me before you jump into ride-or-die mode, alright? I need to know you're okay when I'm out of town, Hood. And me being out of town will be a part of our life together. There's no getting around that fact."

"I'm still trying to get to know my siblings again. You're right about that. And I get what you're saying. To you it's all so strange. To us, it's how we were raised. We come from a different world than you come from. But they're trying to fit in too. It's just gonna take us some time."

Max nodded. He understood that. "Just stay safe," he said to her, "and it'll be okay." And then he kissed her again, but this time far more passionately. He didn't want to let her go.

But he knew he had to. "Take care of

yourself," he said to her as he released her.

"And you take care of yourself," said Hood.

Max smiled. "Oh, I can take care of you and myself with my hands behind my back. Trust and believe."

"And I can take care of myself and you too," said Hood, playing along. "I saved your bacon once, remember?"

"How can I ever forget when you remind me every other day."

Hood smiled, too, and her smile made Max really want to stay. But he had to go. He kissed her once again, got out of the car, and then walked her around to the driver side seat. She got in on the driver's seat.

They gave each other another *I wish I could stay* look, and then she watched him make his way to the plane. She leaned her head against the headrest, with her naturally long lashes almost covering her eyes, and wondered if Max was truly faithful to her on all those business trips he was always going on. And she wondered why he never offered to take her with him. She certainly wasn't going to beg him to. They already were unequally yoked with Max having way more power over her than she ever thought she'd let any man have over her.

It wasn't a great recipe for a marriage,

that was for sure. She constantly wondered how could their marriage ever even work? Especially when she seemed to be the only one worried about it not working. But she loved him so much. She never wanted anything to work more than her marriage to Max. That was why it was going to work. No matter what.

And even after Max had disappeared onto the plane and the doors were closed, she remained where she was. She wouldn't leave until she knew he was safely in the air.

Once his plane took off, she did too.

CHAPTER THIRTEEN

Maxwell Cassidy hurried across the sidewalk in his cashmere coat and well-padded gloves as he braved the freezing temperatures to get inside his Manhattan office building. The doorman hurried to open the door with a smile even Max saw was exaggerated. "Welcome back, Mister C. Welcome back!"

"Thank you, Peter." Max wiped his damp shoes on the provided mat and nodded toward the doorman. "How have you been?"

Peter was surprised that the usually grim man spoke back, and his already grand smile increased. "I been real good, sir. Real good! Trying to stay warm."

"Impossible," Max said, and Peter grinned. Max made his way to the elevator.

Although Max owned the building outright, he rarely used it. Nearly all of the space was rented out to other businesses. He only utilized the top floor whenever he was in town for meetings. Mainly because Cassidy-Minor, a tech firm he inherited from his father, was headquartered in Silicon Valley, and Cassidy Incorporated, which oversaw all of his Cassbar locations and his myriad of other business ventures, was headquartered in his home base of Chicago. New York was just a meeting ground. And given its nasty weather, he couldn't wait to get in and out.

But festive songs were blaring out over the elevator intercom, even if it wasn't a festive time of year, and he found himself singing along as he rode to the top floor. And he kept singing when the doors opened, and he stepped off.

When he saw Jason Bogart, his newly-promoted head of all operations, standing outside of the board room, his singing rose. "'*It's the most wonderful time of the year*,'" Max sung in his best offkey baritone. "'*With the kids jingle belling and everyone telling you - be of good cheer! It's the most wonderful time of the year*!'"

Jason laughed. "Caroling this time of year?"

"That's right," Max said with a smile. "You got a problem with that?"

"No problem over here," Jason said. "Just odd seeing your Grinch-ass all bubbly like this. You're in a good-ass mood."

"Why wouldn't I be? I'm about to sign a deal I didn't even know was possible until a couple weeks ago. And after that, I'm going to be attending a major dinner party where I intend to make even more major deals if those slimy politicians agree to back me at the next city council meeting. And, lest you forget, I have a wonderful bride waiting for me at home too. How can I not be in a glorious mood?"

"Because you're Max Cassidy, that's why. You're never in a glorious mood," Jason said, and Max laughed.

But then Jason looked at Max with a sidelong glare. "That *major* dinner party wouldn't happen to be Mayor Hayden's party, now would it?"

"It would, yes."

"Now that's a switch! You never attend any of his parties, even when it's in your best interest, and he's been inviting you ever since he got in office. You always turn down every invitation as if it's an invite to a leper colony. But suddenly you're going and can't wait to get there?" Then Jason looked at him sideways again. "Are our chances that slim?"

Max nodded. All smiles gone. "And getting slimmer by the day. Opposition like you wouldn't believe."

"Because it'll change the game. If we can pull it off we're talking prime real estate in the heart of Chicago, Max."

"Prime," agreed Max. "It'll become the hub of the city when I get finished with it. But I'm going to absolutely need city buy-in to make any of it happen."

"So far?"

"No deal," said Max. "Nobody's biting any fruit I dangle. I need Hayden to round up the troops and get it done. But we'll see," he added as he moved to open the door of the boardroom. But Jason blocked his path.

Which made Max shake his head with a cynical look on his face. "I knew your ass wasn't standing out here just to greet me. What is it now?"

But Jason didn't respond, which caused Max to look hard at the tall black man who'd been his best friend ever since they were kids in boarding school. It wasn't like Jason to be melodramatic. He was more conservative than Max! "What is it, Jace? I told you I'm on a time crunch. Let's get this show on the road so I can get back to Chicago."

"About this show," said Jason.

"Don't tell me there's another glitch. Don't you dare tell me that. The negotiations are over. I made that clear to our team all day yesterday. If I'm here that means the negotiations are done."

"It's not the negotiations that's the problem. It's one of the *negotiators*."

Max didn't get why any issue with a negotiator would matter to him. The deal, to partner with a top firm in Prague to bring Max's signature Cassbars to the Czech Republic, was finally hammered out late last night by the two teams. He was at his New York office to seal the deal. Not to renegotiate it. "What about one of the negotiators? What's his problem?"

"It's not a him. It's a her."

Max frowned. His usual dour mood was back. "I don't give a good *got*damn if it's a carnival act, do I look like I have time to play games with your ass? Get to the point!"

"One of the negotiators for Albright, the *Closer* for Albright, is Breena Novak, Max."

Max was certain he didn't hear what he'd just heard. And his face frowned a hard frown of disbelief. "*What*? What are you mentioning her name for?"

"Because she's here. In this very boardroom."

Max was beyond stunned. He would not have believed it for anything in this world had it been anybody else telling it to him. But he knew Jason. Jason wouldn't kid about a thing like that. "But she's . . . But I thought she . . ."

"All of us thought it," said Jason. "I was the one who hired that private investigator to quietly try to find her, remember? But that P.I. said it best: when you don't want to be found, it's easy to get lost. She didn't want to be found."

Max opened his suit coat and placed his

hands on his hips. "I don't understand. Do you mean to tell me she's *here*?"

Jason nodded. "She's in that boardroom right now."

"But where has she been all these years?"

"Apparently in Prague."

"That whole time?"

"She's been in the Czech Republic that whole time, yes. At least that's what I was told in the last few minutes when I contacted Albright's CEO."

"Did you tell him--"

"No! Of course not, Max. I just wanted some intel on their Closer, that's all I said to that man. He said she worked her way up to Senior VP and their top deal closer at Albright. You never ran into her because we never had any dealings with that company until this merger. But that's where she landed."

"But that still makes no sense, Jace. What the fuck she's doing in Prague? And what about you? You were there during the negotiations early on and you didn't recognize her?"

"She wasn't there early on. She showed up late last night only because Albright needed her to get it over the finish line. I wasn't there last night. They kept me on speed dial, but I wasn't in the room and didn't give a damn who was closing for Albright. And since she had to be called in, I guess she stayed as the signee on behalf of the company. She has the role for Albright that you have for Cassidy Incorporated today. She's here to seal the deal too."

"But she had to know that Cassidy Inc. is my company. Why would she want to suddenly have something to do with me after the way she left me?"

Jason shook his head. "I don't know, Max. When I walked into that boardroom and saw her sitting there I couldn't believe my eyes. I just walked right back out. To warn you."

Max was duly warned. And so shocked that he could hardly stand up.

Jason saw the effect it was having on him. "We can postpone this."

But the businessman inside of Max leaped out. "No hell we can't. This deal expires midnight tonight if my John Hancock isn't on it, and my John Hancock will be on it." But then Max shook his head. He was stupefied. "And she's *here*?"

"She's here."

"I'll be *got*damn. I wasn't expecting this. This is some shocking news you just laid on me, Jace."

"Shocked me too. Are you kidding? And

I mean the way it went down was just cold. Your wife and daughter killed in that plane crash. You nearly killed. And she decides to ghost you at a time like that? Yes, she knew you were trying to reconcile with Camille instead of divorcing her cheating ass. But you and Breena had been fooling around with each other, off and on, for over a decade before you even met Camille. And yes, I know you never cheated, but all those times you and Camille were separated and sliding toward divorce, you and Breena were tight again and hanging out again. She knew you needed her when Camille and Amber died."

Max sighed. It was hell for him back then. Pure hell. Something he'd been trying to bury ever since. And Breena's sudden disappearance didn't help at all! And now she was back? What kind of bullshit was this?

But there was no getting around it any longer. He had a contract to sign and places to be. "Let's just get this over with," he said to Jason.

"After you," Jason said, opening the door for Max.

Max let out a hard exhale, steeled himself, and then he and Jason walked into the boardroom.

Breena Novak was seated in the center on her team's side of the long table. She was easy to spot. A tall, stunningly gorgeous black beauty with the most remarkable hazel eyes. The only black and only woman on either side of the table. But when Max walked in, both teams stood on their feet, including her. As if he was the center of attention: because he was. Because they all knew without pleasing Max Cassidy there would be no Cassbars anywhere near the Czech Republic.

Max removed his gloves but didn't bother taking off his coat as he sat in the center on his team's side of the table. Once he sat down, everybody else sat down too. He avoided looking at her until they were across the table from each other and he could avoid it no longer.

And when their eyes met, he was shocked. It was as if time had stood still and he was that same broken man, ten years ago, grieving his family, getting over his own injuries and the guilt of being blamed once again for a horrific tragedy, and then waiting for her at their favorite restaurant. And calling her phone repeatedly because she said she'd meet him there. But she never came. And then cursing himself for caring that she didn't come.

He never admitted even to himself how badly he needed her back then. Until now, as he stared across the table at the woman that had disappeared off the face of this earth just when he needed her most.

"Hello, Maxwell." She had that same affectionate smile he remembered so clearly, as if a decade ago was a day ago.

And those feelings, from that time when Jen went missing, from that time when he actually considered divorcing his first wife and marrying her, all came flooding back.

CHAPTER FOURTEEN

For some strange reason, Max felt a sudden sense of dread seeing her again, as if he was in trouble and there was no getting out of it. But he was there to do a job and he did it. His chief negotiator opened up the meeting and began the process. The contracts were put before the principals, namely Max and Breena, for signatures, but as both of them signed they kept taking peeps at each other.

For Breena Novak, it was as if she was transported back to that place when they were young and happy and she was so much in love. He was her first true love and her only true lover. When he married Camille, it devastated her. She planned a murder-suicide she was so devastated. But Max kept her around. Only as a friend mainly, but at least he didn't throw her overboard.

But when the man she privately called her *sponsor* told her what he was up to next, she was overjoyed when she thought it could actually work. Put a little taint on his hood-rat wife while she was still his brand-new bride in a way that would sow just enough doubt in Max's mind. It would get Max to at least wonder if he made the biggest mistake of his life marrying a girl her own mama named Hood. And then Breena would show up to be the familiar alternative while Max was seriously questioning his bride's readiness to be Mrs. Cassidy. And Breena would be all up in his face. Looking like perfection the way she always looked. Still turning heads at thirty-nine years old. She would be *that* bitch. And with the added incentive her sponsor was eager to include, Max would be hers for the taking!

But she was nobody's fool. She knew Max was always a very hard man to read. She knew he never revealed his true feelings about anything. If it was all going to work and her sponsor got what he wanted and she got Max again, everything had to click. She could leave nothing to chance or Max would see right through it. Everything had to work.

But for Max, there were no hidden agendas. He was just stunned. It was all so sudden and so shocking that his feelings were all over the place. Once upon a time he did care deeply for Breena. Once upon a time he did have such strong feelings for the woman that now sat across from him that even he couldn't understand them. And although his feelings for Bree were nowhere near the same level of intensity he felt for Hood, she came as close as any other woman had ever gotten to his heart. Including his first wife.

And to see her now, looking flawless as always, was doing something to his heart. He missed her. He had worried sick about her when she ghosted him. Then he was angry with her and hated her guts for ghosting him. He just knew, back then, he'd do something horrible to her if he saw her again.

And a part of him still held that feeling of deep-seated anger and hatred toward her. But the other part of him felt something completely opposite. And it was that part that was scaring him.

But he stopped focusing on her, and got down to business. Business: something Max had always been able to do no matter what drama swirled around him. He always was about the business. And once all the contracts were signed and a toast of champagne was had by all, the negotiators left. And then Jason, who'd always been suspicious of Bree, reluctantly left too.

But Max and Breena remained where they were.

Max was still unable to believe that she was even there, and that she was still as sun-kissed beautiful as she had been a decade ago: when he last laid eyes on her. As if life had been a breeze for her. While for him, before Hood, it had been a nightmare.

Breena was so inwardly pleased to see Max again that it took all she had to contain her excitement. Of all the men she'd had, before Max and after Max, he was still her gold standard. That strong jawline was what she most remembered. Those terrifying eyes that became soft eyes if he cared about you. She remembered those too. He was a man's man. Somebody she could trust. Somebody she could love. Somebody she still loved so deeply it was killing her!

But she knew Max. He could be a vindictive son-of-a-bitch if you crossed him. She knew she still had a mountain to climb to get him to understand why she left.

Max wanted to know why, alright, but it wasn't *that* why. "Why are you here?" he finally asked her after everybody had gone. "You knew Cassidy Incorporated were in talks with Albright for this merger. You knew I owned Cassidy Inc. Why did you suddenly think it was a good idea to show your face now?"

It wasn't the question she wanted to discuss. But she knew she had to jump that hurdle too. "I'm one of the top closers for Albright," she said.

"Bullshit, Breena." Max wasn't buying it.

"Don't give me that bullshit. That's too pat. Too convenient. Give me a straight answer. Why are you here?"

"Don't talk to me like that, Max."

Max frowned. "I'll talk to you any way I damn well please. Who the fuck do you think you are? You left me!" he yelled, hitting the palm of his hand on the table. "I didn't leave you. You left me!"

It stunned both of them. But Max most of all. Because those emotions were so raw. But how could they be after all those years? Why was he harping on something that had nothing to do with anything anymore?

He attempted to calm back down. "Just answer my question," he said to her. "Why did your ass decide to show up here, at the closing, when you knew I'd be here?"

Breena shook her head. "I don't know why I even bother. But I thought you'd be pleased to see me."

Max frowned. "Pleased to see you? Are you out of your fucking mind? You left me when I needed you most, Bree! My daughter had just died. My wife was dead. *I* nearly died and I was being blamed for that plane crash. And that's when you decide to leave?"

"You told me you were trying to work it out with Camille. You guys were flying to your

119

villa in France to work it out. Why would I be hanging around for that?"

"Because you were my friend!" Max yelled. "A friend I trusted. That's why!"

Breena leaned back in her chair. She knew it would be hard going in. But a part of her was hoping that if he just saw her again it would soften him. But not so. It seemed to have done just the opposite. Which meant, she knew, that he still loved her too. And she had to play on that love. "It wasn't me," she said.

Max tried to understand what she meant by those loaded three words, but he wasn't playing any guessing game with her. All kinds of emotions were locked inside of him, and each of them were trying to come out all at once. But he was pissed with her above all. And that concerned him. He never let anybody he didn't give a damn about piss him off to that degree. Why was he letting Breena do it to him again?

And she wanted to talk in rhymes too? As if he didn't have enough going on inside of him. *And what about Hood*, he thought. Which was his most agonizing thought. Why was he having any emotion at all for this woman sitting in front of him when he had the most precious woman on earth at home waiting for him?

But he was never a man to ignore the truth. He had to ride this horse to get to the other side. "What wasn't you?" he asked her.

"You married Camille. You fought to hold onto your marriage despite her cheating on you with every man moving. All of that effort you gave to Camille. You never gave it to me."

Max frowned again. That couldn't be it! "Camille was my wife. Of course I was going to try to mend my marriage."

"And keep me as what? Your friend in waiting? Your piece on the side?"

"I didn't play that shit and you knew it. You knew our relationship before I ever met Camille."

"I was nineteen years old when we first met."

"And I was twenty," Max shot back. "We were both young. And that's why I told your ass going in don't fall for me. I told you it was a dead-end street. Didn't I tell you that?"

She said nothing.

"Did I or did I not tell you that, Breena?"

Breena reluctantly nodded. "Yes, you told me! But that doesn't mean I understood it."

"Don't pull that innocent shit on me. I was a year older than you and neither one of us were innocent."

"But you were rich!" Breena said forcefully. "That made us unequal."

"My old man was rich. I was a college kid

who didn't have shit back then and you knew it. What I want to know is what are you doing here now?"

She'd heard how he changed into this angry, bitter man after that plane crash. And she could see the change in him. But she needed him now unlike she'd ever needed him before. And nasty or not, she was going to get what she needed.

"What is this about, Breena?" Max asked her again.

And she decided to give as good as she was getting. She decided to be as blunt and nasty as he was. "It's about you divorcing that tramp you married, and marrying me. And marrying me," she added, "with no prenup."

Max looked at her as if she'd lost her mind. Forget a prenuptial agreement! She was talking about him divorcing Hood and marrying her ass when he hadn't even laid eyes on her in a decade? *Was she insane*? On what planet did she think he would even conceive of doing something that batshit crazy?

But he knew she wasn't crazy. Slick as oil, but never crazy. He stared at her as if he was looking at a three-eyed monster. "What would make you think I'd divorce the woman I just married, and marry you? Why would you even suggest such nonsense?"

Breena stood up as if it was much more than a suggestion. "I'll be in New York for two additional days. At the Merrimount. The penthouse suite. Today is Thursday. If I don't hear back from you by end of day Saturday, the deal's off."

Max frowned. "What deal? What the fuck are you talking about, Bree? On what planet am I going to make a deal like that with you?"

But then, to prove on what planet, she dropped the bomb on Max. "I know where Jennifer is," she said.

At first Max just sat there with a puzzled look on his face. But as soon as it registered to him that she'd just said what he thought she'd just said, he jumped up so fast his chair fell backwards. And he nearly went over with it.

CHAPTER FIFTEEN

Max was thunderstruck. His face was in a fixed frown of pure shock. "What are you saying?" he asked Breena. "Are you telling me that you know where Jen. . . . That you--"

"Yes, Max," Breena said. "That's what I'm telling you. I know where she is."

"But how can you . . . What are you talking about? Are you telling me *she's alive*?"

Breena looked at Max with compassion for the first time since they were in that boardroom together. And she nodded her head. "Yes, Max. Jen is alive and well."

Max could hardly believe his ears.

"And you will see her again, and be with her again, if you meet my demands. You have two days," she added, and was about to turn away.

But Max quickly reached over that table and angrily grabbed her by the arm. "You can't tell me something like that and just walk out the door!" He kept his hand on her as he leaped onto that long table and jumped across. He was standing at her side. "Where is she?" Desperation was in his eyes. He was gripping her arm. *"Tell me where she is!"*

"I'm wired, Max. This conversation is being recorded and listened to by men who are not fucking around. So back off!"

But Max only grew angrier. "And I'm not fucking around either!" he yelled. "You're wired? Show me. Jenny's alive? Show me proof she's alive. You think I'll take your word for something like that? You show me proof or I'll tear you apart limb by motherfucking limb for even suggesting that shit to me!"

Breena had never seen Max so out of control. She heard how much he changed after that plane crash. Now she got to see that change in the flesh. And it wasn't pretty. She was scared for her life for the first time ever in Max's presence. And she froze.

Max didn't understand why she would be wired, and who would be listening, but he also knew bullying answers out of her weren't going to work either. He backed up, but only slightly. "Where is she, Bree?" This time he asked with moderation, rather than desperation, in his voice.

But Breena had her own agenda. "If I don't return to my hotel suite without any of your goons following me or in any way harassing me, then the deal is off. I'll go on with my life without you, and you'll go on with your life without Jen.

I promise you that. It's up to you," she added, as she looked down at the hand that was still gripping her too hard.

Max could always tell when Breena was bullshitting him. She had a certain unsettled look he remembered to this day. But her demand and bombshell were no bull. She meant every word.

But she was wired and men were listening? "Show me proof," he said to her.

She had already figured it would come to that, and she didn't hesitate as she unbuttoned her blouse and flung it open. She revealed just how wired she was, with microphone, across her flat stomach. She also revealed she wore no bra.

Then she had the nerve to smile at Max. "Remember those?" she asked him, hoping her taut dark boobs would get his attention too.

But Max was so thrown by her news that he didn't know what she was talking about. He didn't give a fuck about any boobs at a time like this!

When she realized he wasn't the kind of man that could care about something that frivolous after the bomb she'd just dropped, she got serious too. "Are you going to let me leave? Because if you try in any way to hamper me and my freedom, then you'll never see her again.

And there won't be anything I can do about that. There won't be anything you can do about that. It's baked in the cake. I get impeded in any way, you'll be searching twenty more years to find her. They know what they're doing."

"Who are they?" Max asked her.

She looked at him as if he should know better than to expect her to give him any such information.

Then the gangster side of Max began to emerge. Because he, like the woman he married, could be as gangster as he needed to be. "What's to stop me from putting a gun to your head and making a few demands of my own? Like Jenny for you?"

"You can do that," said Breena, "and you'll never see her again. It's not a question of them waiting around for you to torture me. You can torture me all you want. And while you're trying to beat information out of me, they'll be long gone again. Jenny will be long gone again," she added, with regret in her eyes. "And you'll find out I'm as powerless as you are."

Max stared at Breena. And something in her eyes told him she was telling him the truth. But he couldn't take anybody's word for it. Not for this. "Show me proof of life," he said.

Breena could tell Max needed more than what she was telling him. But that wasn't part of the plan. She had to convince him. But she was failing to do so. And her sponsor wasn't going to like that. She didn't know what else to do.

But her hesitation infuriated Max. It felt as if she was toying with him. "Show me proof of life or you'll never walk out of this room, Breena. Show me!" he yelled and grabbed her by the arm so tightly that it scared her.

"He means it!" she yelled to those who were listening over the wire. "Show him proof! He means it!"

And then, within seconds of her cry out, there suddenly was a ding sound on her phone. Max heard it too and released his grip on her. She quickly picked up her phone, pressed the video button displayed, and handed her phone to Max.

Max grabbed the phone and looked at the video. It was a live feed of a door opening. And then the phone's camera somebody held in hand swept around to a sofa where a young woman, sitting Indian-style, was playing a video game on her phone. Max steeled himself as a male's voice said "*turn and face the camera, Jen.*"

When the young woman turned toward that camera and she looked so much like that little girl lost he remembered so well, only she was seventeen years older, it staggered Max.

"What day is it, Jen?"

"You know what day it is."

Her voice still so tiny and *young*. Max could hardly believe it.

"I know what day it is. But I'm asking you to tell me what day it is."

"It's Thursday."

"Today is Thursday. You are correct. And what time is it, Jen?"

"You know what time it is."

"Tell me."

She glanced at her Apple watch. "Eleven-thirteen," she said in a voice that was almost as soft as her childhood voice.

Max glanced at the time on Breena's phone. It was eleven-thirteen. And it was Thursday. But as the young woman placed her hand back on her game controller, Max saw something else. He saw that little dark mark, shaped like a peanut, just above her wrist. He saw her birthmark. It was undeniable!

And then the live feed ended, and the phone screen went to black.

Breena snatched her phone from Max. "Now do you believe me?"

But Max was still standing there as if he was still holding her phone. As if he was still seeing Jen, all grown up now, sitting there. It went beyond belief for him.

He was so shaken that he had to sit down. So he did.

Breena was amazed how Max went from raving lunatic to a man so vulnerable she actually felt sorry for him. But she also knew she had him exactly where she needed him to be. "I said do you believe me now? Do you now understand this is no game?"

Max looked at her. "A game? I see Jen for the first time in seventeen years and you think I could. . ." He couldn't even finish that thought it was so absurd. But his anger restored his sense of reason. "And why would they care if you marry me," he asked her, "if it's not all about you and what you want?"

"You know why," Breena said as she began buttoning back up her blouse. "No prenup, remember?"

Max frowned. "Because of money? If it's only about money I'll pay a ransom --"

"That's not what it's only about," Breena made clear. "That's always a part of it, but that's not half of it."

"Then what is it?" Max was so confused it was hurting him to his core. And he was pleading with her. "What do they want from me? What do *you* want from me?"

"I told you what I want. I want to be Mrs.

Maxwell Cassidy and I will be Mrs. Maxwell Cassidy. That's all I've ever wanted."

"If it's that simple, why did you leave after my wife died? You stood a chance then."

A depressed look appeared in Breena's eyes. A look of profound regret. "I wasn't available then," she said.

Max stared at her. "What's that supposed to mean?"

But she knew, because *he* was listening, that she couldn't say more.

"Okay, I know what you want," Max said. "But what do these people that have Jen want?"

"You'll have to ask them that question, which you won't be able to. So my suggestion? Focus on what I want if you want Jen back."

She was about to leave, but Max stood up and grabbed her wrist. She looked down at his hand on her wrist, and then looked at him. "May I leave?"

Max was unsettled. She was the only link he had to Jen. How could he just let her walk out that door?

She could see his anguish, and her heart went out to him. But he had to understand the stakes. "This is not a test, Max. These men are not playing games with you. If they hear where you are not giving me free passage, it's the end of Jennifer. They don't care what happens to me. I'm just an end-run-around for them. They'll use me as long as they can, and in return I get to be your wife and you get Jen back. But if you don't cooperate, everything's off. You have got to understand that."

"But what am I supposed to be doing for them?"

"Once you divorce Hood Rat Riley and marry me, then you'll know."

"Stop calling her that. And I mean it." He looked Breena dead in her eyes. "Just stop."

It hurt Breena to her heart that he was so willing to stand up for that trick, even at a time like this, when he never stood up for her. "And you'll have Jennifer back," she continued as if he didn't say a word. "If you don't divorce that tramp and marry me, then game over. And *I* mean that." Then she exhaled too. "You have two days."

Max believed her. Instinctively he believed every word she was saying. And he knew he had to let her go.

As soon as he released his grip on her, she grabbed her briefcase and phone and walked on out.

But he also knew, for Jen's sake, he had to keep his wits about him. "Ja-son!" he yelled with a thundering screech. And within seconds, Jason, his go-to for most of his life, came rushing in.

CHAPTER SIXTEEN

"I can't believe I agreed to do this." Rita sat on the backseat of the waiting limousine and began buckling her seatbelt. "I hate going to shit like this."

"We're just helping our kid sister out last minute," Ricky said. "She's always helping us out. And you know how Hood is. She never likes to ask anybody for anything I don't care how desperate she is. For her to ask us to accompany her to this uppity-muck get-together is huge. I'm glad she asked us."

"What get-together? It's no get-together, Ricky. It's a dinner party at the mayor's mansion. A get together is a crab boil in the backyard. This ain't that."

Ricky looked at Rita. Both of them had bruises, although Rita's makeup covered hers very well. But they still looked as if they were as rough as they come, which made Ricky certain he didn't hear her right. "What you mean the mayor's house? Nobody told me nothing about no mayor's house. Are you serious?"

"No, I'm playing. Of course I'm serious! She probably didn't tell you because you didn't ask. Happy-go-lucky Ricky Riley, that's you.

But that ain't me. I don't like being around people like them."

Happy-go-lucky Ricky was more sober now. "We're about to party at the mayor's house? Damn, Reet. I can't believe I agreed to do this either! Can you imagine our hood asses up in the mayor of Chicago's mansion? That's crazy though. And can you imagine Hood all up in a place like that?"

"Are you kidding? I still can't imagine she married a billionaire and is living in *his* mansion, forget the mayor's mansion! But I guess we need to get used to it. They've only been married for a minute, but our baby sister married into another world. And we're in it right along with her. Max has been very good to all of us."

"Yes, Lord. He's the one that reunited us with Hood, and with each other too. But still! The mayor's mansion? I don't know if I'm ready for this, sis."

Rita looked at her brother because she understood. They weren't those kinds of people. And the little she'd already seen of those kinds of people, she knew for certain she never wanted to be anything like them.

And although they were doing it for Hood, that didn't stop Hood from taking her precious time. As if she was doing everything she could to avoid it too.

Before Ricky and Rita got into the limo, they had been inside the house waiting for their baby sister to finally bring herself downstairs. But when Dobbs drove the limo around, they decided to wait in the car hoping that Hood would get the message and bring her ass on. It wasn't working.

"What time is this thing anyway?" Ricky asked as he looked at the time on his iPhone.

"Suppose to start at eight according to what Hood said to me. Why? What time is it?"

"Seven-thirty-five," Ricky said. "But I have a different question."

Rita looked at him. "What's your question?"

"Where the hell is Max?"

"Thank you!" Rita agreed with her big brother. "That's what I'm talking about."

"They literally just got back from their honeymoon and already he's been on the road more than he's been at home. I know he's rich and successful and got to go, go, go to keep them bills paid and them coins coming in, and I respect the man to the utmost for the way he brought our family back together. But dang! He knows how Hood is. She takes everything to heart. She needs him here to show her the ropes. She don't do anything halfway."

"She takes everything so seriously,"

echoed Rita.

"What she know about mayor's mansions and dinner parties and all that uppity-muck stuff? He literally plucked her from straight poverty and made her his wife in no time flat. The least he can do is take a little time to show her how it's done."

Rita pointed a waving finger at her brother. "That's what I'm saying. That's exactly what I'm saying."

"But what is Hood saying?"

"You know how she is. She don't tell me shit. And when I try to tell her, she gets all offended. Max can do no wrong in her eyes and nobody's saying an unkind word about that man, she don't care if it's true or not. She don't give a shit."

"That don't even sound like Hood," Ricky said. "The baby sister I remember is somebody who never takes crap from anybody. That's why her ass had to get out of Chicago all those years ago and move to Utah in the first place." Then he laughed. "I still can't get over that shit. All three of us had to flee the Chi at different times in our lives over some bull we had nothing to do with. I fled to Detroit, which at least made sense. She fled to Utah. You fled to South Dakota where ain't no Negro within a million miles of that place."

"And that's why I made Hood go to Utah, and me and Timmy went to South Dakota. No brothers would ever even bother to look in either one of those two states for us or anybody else."

Ricky laughed. "And my stupid ass fled to Detroit where you can't turn a corner without seeing a hundred brothers. But it worked for me."

"And I didn't say Hood takes Max's bullcrap," Rita said. "She don't take nobody's bull, you're right about that. All I said is that she's devoted to him. She's his ride or die. She'll do anything for that man."

"But will that man do anything for her?" asked Ricky. "And don't look at me like that. I'm just keeping it real. He should be the one going to this big-time dinner party with her since he's making her go. We shouldn't be the ones going with her. What we know? We in the same leaky-ass boat she's in. We don't know shit about no dinner parties, either. We don't know how to maneuver in Max's world either."

"Not yet," said Rita. "But our asses better learn real fast if we expect to roll with Max. Besides, she says he's supposed to meet us over there."

"Then why couldn't she just wait on him, if he's coming anyway?"

Rita was shaking her head. "He needs

the city's approval to build some lakefront development he's looking to build, so he needs to hobnob with the power centers of the city. And it don't get any more powerful than the mayor. That's why Max wants Hood to be there as his representative until he's able to get there. And he wants her there on time."

Ricky shook his head. "All that money that man has and he's still wheeling and dealing like a hustler. Probably why Hood loves him so much. She's got that hustle in her too."

"Here she comes," Rita said as she looked past Ricky.

Ricky looked, too, as their kid sister came out of the main house in her gorgeous, form-fitting above-the-knee cocktail dress with an equally gorgeous whiter blazer thrown across her small shoulders. They smiled at how she was stepping high in her stilettos as if she was born in heels. And her hair, in a fancy up-do, was on-fleek too. Ricky started smiling and snapping his fingers. "Now that's what I'm talking about. Max don't be letting his wife step out looking any kind of way. Everything she's wearing costs a fortune. And that face. That face. That fabulous face!"

"What fabulous?" asked Rita. "She look okay, I'll give her that. But I'm not chopped liver either, you know."

"Compared to Hood you are," said Ricky and Rita, smiling, playfully pushed him. He laughed.

And as Rita looked at Hood again, she smiled too. "You're right. Max got her looking real good. She's no baby anymore."

Dobbs opened the back door of the limousine for Hood, and she sat in between her brother and sister. "What time is it?" she was asking as she sat down.

"You smell great," Ricky said to Hood as Rita glanced at the Rolex Hood wore. Another Max purchase.

"Thanks," Hood responded to her brother.

"It's seven forty-five," Rita said. "According to your watch."

"Oh Lord," said Hood. "Max said he didn't want me to be late. Dobbs?"

Dobbs had just gotten back on the front seat behind the wheel. "Yes, Mrs. Cassidy?"

"Could you go as fast as you can, please? I need to be there by eight."

"Then that's when we shall get there," Dobbs said. He sped off so fast that they all jerked backwards.

"Damn!" said Rita. "Don't get us killed just because Max ordered you to be there on time! Bump Max!"

Ricky was laughing. But Hood was too intense to even crack a smile.

"What's the matter, baby sis?" Ricky asked her. "Stop worrying. You got this."

But Hood didn't feel as if she had a thing. When she was dating Max, he never had her representing him at anything. Now her first time out and it was alone at the mayor's dinner party? The *mayor*? She was nervous as hell.

Ricky could see she was doubtful that she could pull any of it off. He sought to reassure her. "You'll be fine, Hood, you always are. And you look great too. You truly do."

"Thanks, Ricky," she responded. But she still looked as if she just lost her best friend.

"Relax, Hood, damn," said Rita. "It's just a party."

"Yeah, just a party. Just a party at the mayor's house." Hood shook her head. "I'm scared as fuck."

"Then why don't you wait on Max?"

"I told you why. He wants me there and he wants me there on time. He needs the mayor to help him get across that finish line with the city council. I can't wait on anybody. I've got to be there to represent Max."

Rita and Ricky glanced at each other, with Rita giving him an *I told you how devoted to that man she is* look. But they both knew

141

Hood. She'd fly off the handle if either of them said a cross word about Max. They kept their traps shut.

"Where's Timmy?" Hood asked.

Timmy was Rita's now-grown son. "Out with friends. Where else? I told him he could come with us, but he looked at me like I was crazy."

Ricky laughed. "That boy got sense, that's what it is!"

"Which reminds me," said Rita. "How did you manage to get us tickets anyway? Aren't things like this super-exclusive?"

"I asked Max if you guys could go with me since he's running late. He ordered one of his assistants to make it happen. And it happened."

"Thanks a lot," said Rita sarcastically.

"We're thrilled beyond measure," said Ricky, following suit.

Hood smiled, but Rita also noticed how uncomfortable she seemed, and how she kept pulling down on her dress hem. "Will Max approve?" she asked her.

Hood looked at her older sister. "Will he approve of what?"

"That short-ass dress you're wearing."

Hood gave her sister that *are you for real* look they all knew so well.

"He just seems like he could be stupid-jealous, Hood, that's the only reason I'm asking. It's not like it's an out-of-the-blue crazy question. That dress is short. Let's just face it. It's short. I'm just wondering if Max is going to approve."

"And if he doesn't?" Hood asked with that serious, no-nonsense look they also knew.

Ricky laughed. "I told you Hood don't take no mess! And not even from Maxwell Cassidy, thank you very much. Not my baby sister. I told you, Reet, I told you!"

But Rita was always the worrier of the family. She was always the one who had to raise Hood when Ricky left home and never looked back and their mother stayed strung-out on drugs or love or both. And the one thing Rita couldn't get over was the reality that she and her siblings were too dependent on Max. It was Max who hired detectives to find them and bring them back together as a family. It was Max who gave Ricky the job as one of his regional managers-in-training and Rita the job as a senior VP-in-training. And that was concerning to Rita. Because she knew, if he and Hood were to ever break up, he'd kick them out right along with their sister. That was the kind of control Max had over all three of their livelihoods that Rita would never be comfortable with.

She looked at Hood as Dobbs sped through the streets of Chicago. "Have you had a chance to think about the proposal I told you about?"

Hood wasn't trying to hear anything about that tonight. "Yes, Rita."

"And?"

"No."

Rita frowned. "Why not, Hood?"

"Because I'm not doing that."

"But we gotta have something separate going on that won't have us dependent on Max so much. If we can get our own thing going on the side--"

But Hood wasn't about to allow her sister to drag her into anything outside of her marriage. "I said no, Rita. I'm not doing any of that slick shit behind my husband's back that you're talking about. And after all he's done for all of us too? You can forget that."

"But what if it don't work out, Hood? Me, you, and Ricky all depend on that marriage of yours working out. Because if it doesn't work, guess what? We're all out on our asses no matter which way the cookie crumbles."

"And then we'll find our own jobs and make our own way," Hood said firmly. "We been doing that all our lives and we'll just have to do it again. Save what money you can for these rainy days you're so worried about is all I can tell you."

"He's not paying us top dollar, Hood, and you know it. We'll be getting trainee money for a whole year before we start making any real money. You know how Max is."

"Just keep me out of it, Rita, and I mean that. Because I'm telling you now like I told you before: I'm not doing any of that under-the-table side-street secret shit behind my husband's back. I'm not doing it!"

Rita's frustration with her sister was at a boiling point, but she maintained her cool. Because Hood could boil over too, and then it could get ugly. Because Rita knew better than anybody that if you poked Hood the wrong way, she had a worse temper than her and Ricky combined!

But Rita still believed her way made sense. "You're taking this ride or die shit too far, little girl," she said. "But keep on with your bad self. When that man show your ass what time it is, you'll wake up."

Hood looked at Rita. "What's that supposed to mean?"

"You're young, Hood. You're still in your twenties."

"What do you mean in my twenties like I'm twenty-one? I'm twenty-nine."

"And Max is a forty-year-old man. And he's no young forty either. He's a man with more experience than all three of us put together, and me and Ricky got some serious experience."

"Yes Lord," said Ricky.

Rita continued. "Max is a man of the world who's done some things I guarantee would blow even my mind. I hate to tell you this, sis, but the chances of your marriage working with a man like that are slim to none. Let's be real here."

Hood had already concluded that it was a great chance she and Max wouldn't make it. He had too many temptations tossed his way on the regular she was certain. And what did she really bring to the table? She was barely educated, been broke all her life, and had just lost the nothing job she did have when he met her. And people could tell her all day long how pretty she was and how desirable she was to men, but when she looked in the mirror she didn't see all that. All she saw was that little lonely girl who was despised by her own mother. What loving mother would name their loving daughter *Hood* on purpose? She saw pain and fear that she'd been able to disguise as toughness and courage when she looked in that mirror.

But that was why she was determined to make her marriage work. That was why she was determined to do nothing to ever make Max leave her. He was the only man to ever love her. The only one. By any means necessary she was holding onto that love. And no scheme of Rita's was changing that fact.

But Rita believed in her heart of hearts that they had to get something out of this deal before it all went south on them. Because unlike Hood, she'd been with a lot of men in her life, and she knew the games they played. And if a man like Maxwell Cassidy was faithful to Hood the way Hood was faithful to him, she'd eat those stilettos Hood wore.

But how could she get stubborn Hood to see it too? "What I'm trying to get you to see, Hood, is that we need options for ourselves."

"I told you no, Reet. You're wasting your breath. No."

"But if you only just--"

"No, Rita, damn!" Hood was stunned she was still harping on that when she was trying to get herself together to face those high-class folks that would judge her all night long.

Rita was so frustrated that she turned to their big brother, whom she knew agreed with her plan. "Ricky, can you please talk some sense into that child?"

But Ricky wasn't trying to get in between their mess. "Ricky? Who's Ricky?"

Ricky smiled and then looked away from both of his beloved sisters. And his smile left. Because he knew it, too, that they were all hanging by a slender thread. Maxwell Cassidy's thread.

CHAPTER SEVENTEEN

Max's jumbo jet tore through the skies as it made its way back to Chicago. Jason sat across from Max as the crew remained up front. Thanks to that sudden appearance by Breena Novak and the fact that Max wanted to hang around to see what his security team could find out, they were flying back super late. But Max had already phoned Hood and told her to get to the mayor's house without him. He'd be there when he could get there.

But the tension on that plane was sliceable. Jason had rarely seen the boss so unhinged. But Jason was unhinged too.

It had been an earth-shattering meeting with Breena. Jenny was still alive, and the only way Max could ensure that she was returned to him was if he divorced Hood and married Breena. It was insanity on top of craziness to Jason. But Breena was wired. And Max saw Jenny on a live feed. It was all so real. And he only had two days to make up his mind!

When he called him into that boardroom after Breena had gone, Jason could see Max's anguish.

"You okay?" was the first thing he asked

him.

"Get a detail on Breena right now," Max ordered. "I want to know where she's going and who she's going with every second of the day."

Jason quickly phoned the security detail waiting outside of the building. "A subject is coming out of the building as we speak," he said as he described Breena down to the fur coat and boats she wore. "Let me know as soon as you eyeball her."

It took a couple minutes, but the detail chief came back onto the phone. "We see her now, Boss," he said.

"Stay out of sight," Jason said, "but tail her."

"What about Mr. Cassidy? Do we keep a man back to be with him?"

"I'll be with him. You take the full crew with you and keep tabs on her. Just make sure she doesn't know you're tailing her. But do not let her out of eyeshot."

"She's staying at the Merrimount hotel," said Max. "The penthouse suite."

"She's staying at The Merrimount," said Jason into the phone, "in the penthouse. You won't be able to access her once she goes inside, but guard every exit."

"Will do, Boss," said the detail chief, and Jason ended the call.

Then he looked at Max. "What's this about?" he asked him.

Max was pacing the floor as if he was a wounded animal.

"What is it, Max? You look like you saw a ghost."

"Oh yeah? I wish that was all I saw."

That response surprised Jason. And his voice revealed his concern. "What is it?"

Max finally stopped pacing and looked at Jason with grave distress in his eyes. And told him all Breena had told him.

Now, on the plane heading back to Chicago with Max, it was a question of what now. "What are you going to do about it?" he asked him.

But Max didn't answer. Which Jason knew he wouldn't. "I just don't want to see Hood get hurt," Jason added.

Max looked at his best friend as if he was offended. Any other day and he would have cussed his ass out. Why would he hurt his own wife? But he didn't say a word. He just looked back out of the plane's window.

"You've got to think of Hood in this situation too," Jason said, refusing to be intimidated. "Hood comes first. I know that's hard to hear with what Bree dangled in front of you about how to get Jenny back, but it's got to be your starting point." It was hard for Jason to even say. But he felt it had to be said. "You hear me, Max? Hood comes first. Right?"

But Max wasn't trying to hear him. He was staring out at the wild blue yonder watching the clouds float by and was in such a daze he had even lost track of where he was. It felt as if some terrible trick had just been played on him at the worst possible time in his life. He'd just gotten married. He hadn't been married two months yet and she decided now was the time to come at him that way? It was cruel as cruel could be. But that was Breena.

And then she dropped that bomb on him. A bomb that Max didn't see coming and didn't know how to even respond to. When she realized how paralyzed he truly was, she told him not to answer her right away, and to think about it. *To think about it*, she said. As if it was as simple as a thought! And then she got up, gathered her gear up, and left.

And Max couldn't move. He still felt frozen in place. And all of his concern wasn't even about Breena. Or about him. It was about Jenny. And Hood.

His precious Hood. A woman with a platinum heart who *felt* everything. A woman who did everything in her power to please him. Who loved him unconditionally.

How in the world was he going to tell Hood that there was a sacrifice to be made, and she was it?

Jason could talk until he was blue in the face, but Max wasn't hearing a word he had to say. Because everything had changed. His world as he knew it had just been tossed upside down. And he had no clue how to right this plane. This runaway plane that was determined to take him down once again.

CHAPTER EIGHTEEN

The limo pulled up to the stately mansion and Dobbs assisted the siblings out of the backseat.

It wasn't as gorgeous nor as big as Max's estate, but it was grand. So grand that it had Ricky all smiles. "Are we the only poor folks in this world that Max knows?" he asked.

But Hood and Rita were too terrified to brush it off with jokes. "I feel like a hood rat at a White House picnic," said Hood.

"And Trump is the president," added Rita.

Ricky laughed at that too. Although the sisters weren't joking.

Both Ricky and Rita stood on either side of their baby sister, as if they were holding her up. Because they knew they were only there to be her support.

"Before we go in," Hood said, and both siblings looked at her.

"Before we go in what?" asked Rita.

"Call me April."

Even Ricky looked concerned. "April? Your middle name?"

"Yes."

"Why?" asked Rita.

"Because I don't want them laughing at Max."

Rita frowned. "Why would they laugh at Max because of the name your mama gave to you?"

"Because I don't want these people thinking Max married some, you know, some hood rat."

"But he did marry a hood rat. Real talk," Ricky said. "And your mama did name you Hood. Real talk. So what's the problem? You scared of these rich white folks?"

"I'm not scared of anybody! You know me better than that. But I don't want them to turn against Max on account of me."

"Max is a billionaire. Nobody turns against a billionaire. So stop worrying so much. You're getting just like Rita!"

"Just call me April." There was plea in her eyes. "Please."

She could tell neither one of her siblings liked it, but they gave her some grace. Especially Rita, who understood where Hood was coming from. "If that's what you want," she said, "that's what we'll do."

Hood nodded. "I knew I could count on you guys. Thanks."

Then Rita exhaled. "Ready?"

"May as well be," Hood said and they

began walking toward the entrance. Hood was staring at the other arrivals in their furs and jewels and how they all were so white and so old and so unlike anybody Hood or her siblings were accustomed to spending their evenings with.

"These people are like sophisticated giraffes," Rita said as they stood at the back of the line to go inside, "and we're like mangy dogs coming up in there."

Ricky, grinning, started singing that Anselm Douglas/Baha Men song only for his sisters to hear: "*Who let the dogs out? Who, who, who, who - Who let the dogs out? Who, who, who, who, who?*"

But even that wasn't enough to put a smile on his sisters' faces. They were just too out of place.

But they all knew they had better get accustomed to this kind of place. They were in Max's world now.

The line moved briskly, as the greeters let the people in with just a smile and *have a nice time* formalities. Until Hood and her siblings got up to that door.

"May I help you?" one of the greeters asked. The other greeter let those behind Hood and her siblings go on ahead of them.

But the siblings all looked at the greeter.

"May you help us? No," said Hood. "We don't need any help."

Hood was about to walk on by, too, but the greeter stopped her. "What I mean to say," the woman said with what the siblings took as one of those fake Karen smiles, "is what are you doing here?"

"The same thing everybody else is doing here," said Hood. "This is a party. We're here to attend the party."

"I doubt if that's accurate," said the woman. "Do you have your invitations?"

Ricky and Rita looked at each other with that *here we go* look on their faces, but Hood frowned. "Why you got to see our invitations? You let everybody else walk right on in. Why were they allowed to walk right on in?"

"I'll give you three guesses," said Rita. "And every one begins with that big fat W."

"What's the problem here?" An impatient-looking white man came up to the door and asked.

"There's no problem," said Hood. "I just don't understand why she's treating us differently that everybody else."

Hood knew why. She was born in America, she definitely knew why. But that didn't mean she had to lay down and take it.

"Step aside please," the man said as

another old white couple walked up and was allowed uninterrupted passage inside.

"Ain't this some bull?" Rita said.

"If you just show your invitations that'll take care of it," the man said.

"Let's go, Hood," said Rita, pulling her sister's arm. "Forget this shit."

But Hood snatched away. She couldn't just leave. This was a big deal to her husband. "May I speak with the mayor or his wife, please?"

When Hood made that pronouncement, Ricky and Rita looked at her shocked that she would go there. Then they looked at the man.

The man seemed to turn a couple shades of red, as if he was beginning to doubt his superiority over them, but then he figured she was bluffing anyway. But just in case she wasn't? "Just one moment," he said and left to go and get one of the two people Hood requested.

Rita pulled Hood aside. "What are you doing? Do the mayor or his wife know you?"

"Our marriage was in the papers."

"That don't mean shit in Chicago, Hood. Oprah is from Chicago. They're used to billionaires around here."

But Hood didn't like going about it this way, either, but she wasn't leaving. They'd love to see her leave.

Then an older white woman came to the door. But she looked even more dour than the white man looked. Especially when she saw Hood and her siblings. "Yes? I am quite busy. What do you want?"

"I want to register an official complaint against your greeters."

The greeters glanced at each other with smug smiles on their faces.

"And you are?" the woman asked Hood.

"And you are?" Hood asked the woman.

"I'm Penelope Hayden. That's who I am. But who are you to register a complaint at my dinner party? This is by invitation only."

"My husband was invited, and we are under his invitation."

"Who is your husband? Him?" She nodded toward Ricky. "Because we do not do three additional people under one invitation. That's absurd."

"This is Ricky my brother. He's not my husband," said Hood.

The woman's look became less certain. "Then who is your husband, if you don't mind my asking?"

"My husband is Maxwell Cassidy, and he--"

Penelope, shocked, suddenly produced

a grand smile on her face. "Oh, Mrs. Cassidy! So nice to see you. I was waiting for your arrival. Come in, please. You and your group. Please come in!" Then she looked admonishingly at the greeters and the man over them. "What's wrong with you? How dare you keep Maxwell Cassidy's wife waiting like this! Please come in," she said again, to Hood and her siblings.

Rita and Ricky looked at those greeters with a smug smile on their faces as they followed their kid sister inside the mansion.

"Kid can handle herself," Ricky whispered as they walked across the threshold.

"And then some," added Rita, equally impressed.

But Hood knew it was nothing to be impressed about. Whenever she felt under attack, she came out swinging. That was in her nature. That would never change.

"It's so good of you to make it," the older woman said. "We have been trying to get your husband to one of our parties for a coon's . . . for ages! Let me introduce you to my husband," she added as she escorted Hood and her siblings across the room, to Mayor Hayden and the group that surrounded him.

But as soon as the mayor's wife released Hood and her siblings to the mayor and his group, Penelope's group of girlfriends pulled her aside to get the scoop directly from the horse's mouth.

"Is that her?" asked one of them.

Penelope nodded as they all continued to stare at Hood. "She's the youngest one in that group."

"Who are the others with her?"

"Her sister and her brother, apparently."

"Max love going over to the dark side, doesn't he?" They giggled. "And she's young."

"And not bad looking," said another friend. "In fact, she's quite attractive, if I may say so myself. But she looks so . . . so . . . *mean*."

"Darling, they all look that way." More laughter.

"But I was hoping we could finally have a pipeline into Max's coffers with his new bride. We could get her to join the club and become besties with her and get her onboard with all of our charities. But we can't invite somebody like *that* to join our club. We'd be kicked out for even attempting such an insult!"

"And I know so many gorgeous girls who would have given their right arms to be Mrs. Maxwell Cassidy," said another one. "Yet he picks *her*?"

"Max has always dabbled on the dark side," said Penelope. "That's what many people don't know about him. He likes black women. He only married Camille because she was with child."

One of her friends was shocked. "Was she?"

"That was the prevailing wisdom back then, yes," said Penelope. "But don't worry about this one. She's no Camille."

"I agree wholeheartedly," said another friend. "That marriage won't last a year I guarantee it."

"A year?" Penelope seemed offended. "You are far too optimistic, dear. I wouldn't give it six months! In fact," she said with a smile as she looked across the room, "I have invited someone that will easily knock several additional months off of that prognostication."

"Oh yes? And who did you invite with that kind of power?"

The mayor's wife smiled and nodded her head. "Does Alan Browne ring a bell?" she asked, and the other ladies, looking across the room as well, smiled that knowing smile too. They'd all, to a woman, had their *Al Browne* nights.

CHAPTER NINETEEN

For the next few hours, Hood was bored to tears. Dinner should have been served by now, she thought, because she was starved. But it wasn't that kind of dinner. It was all about networking and leaving your business card and asking her if Max could do this favor for them or that favor for them as if she was going to advocate for those rich fools she didn't even know. And although she kept it polite, she wasn't going to put on any fake smiles or laugh at any unfunny jokes or agree to tell Max anything. He asked her to be there, and she was there. The selling job would have to be up to Max.

But not unsurprising to Hood, Rita and Ricky were far more relaxed than she was. They had those outgoing personalities that knew how to blend in. Or at least pretend to blend in. Ricky had even managed to talk and smile his way into the billiards room for a gentlemanly game of pool, and Rita didn't have to do much to get several men talking to her. The women didn't seem interested. But their husbands did!

Hood was momentarily alone, taking a

breather from all of the networking, when she saw Max walk into that house.

And when Max walked in, looking so debonair in his head-to-toe Armani; looking so gorgeous to Hood that she still was having a hard time believing she was his wife, she didn't quite know what to do. But it was true. He was her husband. She was his wife. And she was thrilled to see him again.

And as soon as Max walked in it was as if the party had just begun. The mayor, his wife, and every other big wig were tripping over each other getting to Max. And he knew how to play the game. He was a great glad-hander and back slapper too. He was in his element.

But when he glanced over at Hood, the hairs on the back of her neck stood up. Because she knew that look he gave her. And it was not the look of love. But the look of shame. Of *his* shame.

Hood wanted to hurry over to him and ask him what happened, but she couldn't do it. Because there was no disguising that look. She knew that look. And she knew, based on that look, that something terrible had happened that was going to rock their marriage. Somehow Hood could feel it.

Another sign was the way he didn't rush over to greet his still-newlywed wife the way most husbands would do, but continued to hold court with his admirers. Hood watched him gladhand and backslap and do what he had to do to get what he wanted from those people. Because Max was like that too. He loved wheeling and dealing. He loved when deals came together. But Hood was anxious to know what that look was about? What happened in New York? Because something happened. Or would he pretend there was nothing to see here and all was well?

It would break Hood's heart if he played that kind of game with her.

"I see the boss man back."

Hood glanced over her shoulder. Rita had just walked up. "Don't call him that," she said to her big sister.

"Why not? He is my boss. He is the boss man."

"Whatever, Rita."

Rita looked at Hood. "What's wrong?"

Hood didn't respond.

Now Rita was really concerned. "What has he done now?"

Hood frowned. "He hasn't done anything. Why do you always go straight to the negative?"

"Because he's a man and that's where men live: in the negative. I just go where they are."

Hood looked at her. She had a drink in her hand and seemed a little tipsy to Hood. "Are you drunk?"

"Of course I am." She grinned. "And about to get laid too."

"Laid? I thought you said you hated Republicans. This place is crawling with them."

"I didn't say I was about to vote for any of these fools. I said I was about to get laid by one of these fools. And his politics isn't what I'm after." Rita grinned again.

Hood rolled her eyes. "I thought you used to only sleep with the brothers."

"I was in South Dakota all those years, Hood. How many brothers you think were hanging around for me to sleep with? I'll give you an easy guess: zero. I been fooling around with white boys for years. And you know what I found?"

"What?"

"Ain't no difference. Not in bed, not in anything. They're assholes too. Even bigger assholes when you consider their fragile egos."

"Then why do you bother with them?"

Rita frowned. "Why do you think? Do I look like a nun to you?"

"That wasn't quite the profession I was thinking about," Hood said and smiled, which caused Rita to laugh out loud.

"But seriously," Rita said, "why the long face? Max did something wrong?"

Hood's smile slowly dissipated. "I don't know yet."

"But you've got that old Hood feeling?"

Hood nodded. "Yes."

"Damn," said Rita, looking at Max. "It's starting already? Y'all just got married and it's already started? And you don't think it makes perfect sense for us to get our own thing going asap?"

"Don't start."

"We need to protect ourselves, Hood."

"Then protect yourself. But keep me out of it."

Rita shook her head. "I give up," she said. "Max got you wrapped so tight around his finger he's squeezing the life out of you."

Hood didn't say anything. Rita knew nothing about Hood's life or how tough it had been for her after she fled Chicago. Max had literally rescued her up out of the mud. And he was Hood's ticket out and she was going to work her ass off to make that ticket successful. Even though she'd never seen a successful marriage in her life. Even though she had to figure it out as she went along.

But Rita was looking across the room as

a tall white man motioned at her. "Okay, gotta go," she said as she handed Hood her drink. "He's telling me to meet him outside."

But Hood grabbed her arm as she was about to walk away. "Rita, are you serious? What are you doing?"

Rita looked at her. "I told you what I was doing."

"Why would you go with a man who doesn't even respect you enough to come and get you and escort you out of this house?"

A sad look appeared in Rita's eyes. "Why do you think, Hood? I ain't got no billionaire waiting to rescue me. Ain't no knight in shining armor gonna sweep me off my feet. Men been treating me like this my whole life. This is all I'm used to. I either get this or don't get shit. That's why I go." Then she snatched her arm from Hood's grasp and walked away.

Hood's heart sank for her sister. She was the one most likely to succeed in their family. Hood was the one least likely. Hood had no idea how it could have flipped so completely.

But as she watched her sister leave and thought about it even more, she suddenly felt a hand on her shoulder. When she turned around, she saw a black man around the same age as she was standing just behind her. She was so surprised that she actually smiled.

"Hey," she said.

"Hey. I thought I was the only unicorn up in here."

Hood laughed. "Not quite. My sister and my brother are here too. Or at least my sister *was* here. I think my brother's in the billiards room."

The young man extended his hand. "I'm Al Browne by the way. Not to be confused with the incomparable Al Green."

Hood laughed again and shook his hand. "I'm Hood," she said before she realized she was saying it. "April," she corrected herself.

"Too late," Al said with a laugh. "You slipped and gave me your nickname. It'll be Hood from here on out."

Hood wasn't her nickname but the real name her mother named her. But that wasn't his business. And he spoke as if he was certain there would be a *here on out*, which was ridiculous. But he certainly was one of the best-looking men she'd ever seen around anywhere with his flawless golden-brown skin and heavy hazel eyes. "Are you a friend of the mayor's?" she asked him.

"Of the mayor's? No. But I am a friend of his son. We were president – me- and vice president – his son – of the college Republicans when we were at Northwestern together."

Hood knew Northwestern was a school near Chicago, but that was all she knew about it.

"Good to see a three-fer here too," Al said.

Hood looked at him. "What's a three-fer?"

"Young, gifted, and black."

Hood found him amusing, but very presumptuous too. "Who says I'm gifted?"

"Aren't you?"

"No."

"Oh, but you are, my dear."

"Oh yeah?"

"Oh yes. Trust me I know these things. You are most definitely the most gifted woman in this house. You know why?"

"Why?"

"Because you're the most beautiful."

He was full of shit and Hood knew it. But he was refreshing too. She'd been around so many older people since she met Max, and her siblings were older too, that it felt good to talk to somebody her own age. So she decided to just go with it. Max hadn't bothered to even come and see about her since he entered that home. Why should she pine away waiting for him?

But across the room where Max was surrounded as if he was a rock star, he kept taking peeps at Hood. And who, he wondered, was the young man with her? A very attractive, well-built young man he also noticed. And they seemed so chummy with all of the laughing and smiling. But when the young man placed his hand on her lower back while they were in the throes of another one of their laughing fits, Max had had enough.

"Excuse me," he said while the mayor was in the midst of talking to him and the others in the group about his first foray into politics. It was so rude of Max that everybody looked as if they couldn't believe he walked away. But Max didn't care what they couldn't believe. He made his way to Hood.

Even before he got all the way over to the twosome, he was already asking his question. "What's so funny?" he was asking them.

Al looked at him with a *who is this guy* look on his face. "Pardon?"

Max made it all the way up to them. "What's so funny?" he asked again.

"And how would that be your business?" Al quickly blurted out.

Max immediately began getting into Al's personal space. "This is my wife you're giggling with. That's how it's my business. *She's* my business."

But Hood quickly pushed Max back. "This is my husband, Al," she said to the young man. "And he's tripping."

Max looked at her as if he wanted to slap her. But even Hood knew it was more about that shame in his eyes. He wanted her to be just as bad as he was, but he knew she wasn't.

She looked at Al. "Could you give us a moment?"

Al looked over at Max again. How could somebody like Hood end up with some asshole like that guy? "Sure thing," he said to her, gave Max another hard look, and then walked away.

But he walked right into the mayor's son Blake. Who was grinning. "He told you," he said.

"Fuck him," said Al.

"You know who he is right?"

Al actually didn't. "Who?"

"Maxwell Cassidy."

Al still had no clue.

"He keeps a low profile, to be certain," said Blake. "But you ever been to a Cassbar?"

"I think so yeah. It's like Hooters, right?"

"Right."

Then Al's face finally showed that he got it. "*He owns Cassbar*? But the guy that owns Cassbar is a billionaire!"

Blake smiled and nodded. "And you were just trying to hit on his wife. Better hope she doesn't tell him who you are and where you work."

Al handed Blake his drink. "Man, I'm out of here. Your mama trying to set me up! No way am I fooling around with a billionaire's wife, is she on drugs? I'm out," he said. Blake laughed, but Al took off.

But Max and Hood didn't have that option. They were now face to face. And that look of shame Hood had correctly picked up on dominated Max's entire countenance.

"What happened?" Hood asked him.

He couldn't do it. He was still processing it himself. How could he just come out and tell her something like that when he couldn't handle it himself? And as that look of shame combined with adject distress, Max pulled her into his arms. "Nothing," he said to her, holding her. "Nothing at all."

Hood's heart dropped. Because she knew he was lying to her. Not only had something terrible happened while he was away from her, but it changed him so much that he was willing to lie to her about it. Something she truly believed, in the little time she'd known him, he'd never done. Their entire relationship was built, she thought, on being brutally honest with each other.

And she was determined to make certain it remained that way.

She pulled back from Max with a look so determined that even Max took notice. "What happened?" she asked him again.

But he said nothing again.

"Max? What is it? And don't you dare tell me nothing."

Max stared at the woman he loved, as he couldn't stop thinking about the woman that had left him, and he knew there was no sweeping that kind of burden under anybody's rug.

But Max looked around. He wasn't about to discuss it at a politician's house. He looked at Hood again. "Let's go home," he said to her.

And Hood, already knowing this was serious business, didn't object in the least.

CHAPTER TWENTY

It wasn't until Dobbs had driven them home, Max had prepared drinks for them, and they were seated side by side on the verandah did he finally tell her what happened seventeen years ago, and how, while his kid sister was downstairs being snatched, he was upstairs fooling around like the irresponsible jerk he was back then.

But Hood was stuck on the first part. "Your sister was kidnapped and never found? You never told me that. You never told me your sister was kidnapped."

"It's not something I discuss."

Hood found that an odd thing to say. Had it been one of her siblings, that would have been the first thing she said. "You said you have a lot of half-siblings because your father slept around, but you never said anything about one of them being kidnaped."

"She wasn't one of them. She was my kid sister Jennifer."

"So she wasn't a half-sister?"

"No." Then Max exhaled. "She's alive,

Hood. I saw her, on video, for myself."

Hood sat upright. "After seventeen years she's alive? Where has she been?"

"I don't know. Breena claimed she doesn't know either. She says the people who have her aren't fucking around. They have her wired."

"But what did she say? What does she want?"

Max hesitated. Then he just said it. "She wants me to divorce you and marry her."

Hood was so stunned she could hardly contain herself. And he said it as if that wasn't the issue. As if that wasn't the big problem. "She *what*? And what did you say?"

"What was I going to say to shit like that? It's insanity."

Hood agreed. "It's crazy." But somehow she was hoping he would have taken such a crazy idea off the table.

She steeled herself for more.

"Then she told me," Max said, as if he was steeling himself to say it. "She told me if I didn't divorce you and marry her, then I'd never see Jen again."

Hood stared at Max. She understood immediately what that meant.

Max leaned his head back. He was unable to contain his anguish. "I wanted to torture her into telling me. I was ready to do whatever it took to get her to tell me. But she was wired. And they heard the entire conversation. And if I didn't let her go, they'd take Jen away for another seventeen years. Or do her grave harm."

Hood had expected to hear many things, but nothing like that. "And you don't know who has her?"

"No.."

"But . . . Was there a ransom back then?"

"Yes. And my father paid it too. But they took the money and never produced Jen. They took the money and ran."

Hood could only imagine the pain he and his parents had to experience.

"And it was all my fault."

Hood shook her head. "No it wasn't either. Whoever took your sister, it was their fault."

But Max knew better. Had he not been so damn horny, he would have been downstairs to save her.

"My family was never the same again," said Max. "My father died in a car crash shortly after that, and my mother died of a heart attack within that same year too. They never recovered from that. *I* never recovered from that."

"*Oh, Max!*" Hood's heart was breaking for him. She got up from her seat and sat on the lounger beside him. She wrapped both arms around him and laid her head on his shoulder.

"We hired so many private detectives to look for her it was insane. Sometimes twenty different investigative teams were looking for her. I got a team together and looked everywhere too. Jason took a leave of absence from law school and got a team together and was looking everywhere with his group. But it was as if she disappeared off the face of the earth. And I couldn't talk about that. I never talked about that. But I still, to this day, have investigators on retainer who are supposedly still searching for my baby sister. But they never have anything to report year after year after year. Seventeen years and counting. And then Breena shows up."

"With her ultimatum."

Max nodded. "Yes."

Hood hated to ask it, but she needed to know. "She's in love with you?"

Max wasn't trying to hear that. "She says she is. I don't know. I don't fucking care. I just want my sister back."

Hood snuggled against him. She understood that. "What do we do?"

"I have two days to decide. She's holed

up in a hotel in New York. I have people on her."

"And then what?" Hood asked him point blank.

"And then I have to decide. I have to make a decision."

"But why does she have to marry you for you to get your sister back?"

"I think that's only a part of it. I don't think that's the main reason."

"Then what's the main reason?"

"She says I won't know until I divorce you and marry her, with no prenup."

Hood couldn't bring herself to ask if he was going to go through with it. She just couldn't do it.

Hood looked at Max and realized that that look, that same look she saw at the party, wasn't a look of shame at all. It was a look of *pain*. Searing pain. "What if it's true, Hood? What if she can bring my sister back home to me?"

Hood understood the implications. "But isn't there something you can do to make her cooperate? The FBI can---"

"No, they can't. And I can't either."

"But why not?"

"Because if anybody lays a hand on her, or silence her or make her disappear, or torture her in any way, the people that have my sister will either kill her, or leave with her again."

"According to this Breena person?"

"Even if that's all bullshit, Hood, what am I supposed to do? I can't risk my sister's life all over again. And I'm not going to risk it."

It was worse than Hood could have imagined. "What can we do?" she asked him again.

But Max had no answers. He had people on the case, from Prague to New York and Chicago too. But they weren't finding out anything either. It was early days and tough decisions had to be made. Devastating decisions.

He pulled Hood closer against him and kissed her on the top of her head. "It'll work out in the end," he said to her. But even he didn't believe it.

CHAPTER TWENTY-ONE

Hood sat in the bathtub trying with all she had to stop thinking about the load Max had dropped on her. His long-lost kidnapped sister might be alive and his ex-lover knew where she was? How was he not going to act on that? And the only way that ex-lover was going to give up the goods was if Max divorced Hood and married the woman? Hood didn't know how to even process such news!

She knew her marriage to Max was going to be an uphill climb that she was going to have to give her all to keep. She knew that going in. But how could she fight against his long-lost sister? And his long-lost lover? How could anybody fight against that?

She got out of the tub and grabbed a towel. She felt like going straight to bed. Just forget everything and go straight to bed. But she knew she wouldn't be able to sleep a wink.

As she walked out of the bathroom still drying off, she stopped suddenly when she saw Max lying, still in the same suit he wore at the party, on top of the bed. Before he realized she was there, she could see his eyes staring up at the ceiling as if his mind was a million miles away. The news was affecting him far worse than it was affecting her, because he had everything on the line both ways: his marriage and his kid sister. And here she was just worrying about herself.

She sighed, and in so doing caused Max to look her way. When he saw that she was no longer in the bathroom, and he saw that look on her worried, expressive face, he reached out his hand to her. "Come here," he said to her.

Hood at first hesitated, as if she was afraid that he had already made up his mind and it wasn't going to be good news for her. But he wouldn't do that to her even for his sister.

Or would he?

She went to the bed and he pulled her naked body on top of him. And he wrapped his arms around her. "Cold?" he asked her.

She should have been, given her exposure, but she wasn't. His big, loving arms were sufficient. "No."

"You're shaking."

That was a surprise to Hood. "I am?"

"You're worried, aren't you?"

Why did he keep asking her that? She leaned up and looked at him. "I'm concerned, Max, yes. I'm not gonna lie to you. It's scary as hell what you told me. And your poor sister could still be in danger if you don't go along with what that lady wants."

"I don't want you worrying about that, Hood. I pay men top dollar to worry about that. You let me worry about that."

Hood said nothing. How could she not worry? That would be like telling her to not think about the elephant in the room. How could she not think about it?

Max could feel her anxiety. His was through the roof too. But he knew he had to comfort Hood. She always wore her feelings on her sleeve. She worried about every single thing. "You trust me, don't you?" he asked her.

"Yes," Hood said without hesitation. Then she looked at him. When he said nothing else, she laid her head back on his chest.

Max didn't know what to really say to her. All he could think about was Jenny and what he was going to do about that situation. But Hood was now and would always be his number one priority. He had to remind her of that fact. "Don't you worry about us, Hood. You hear me? We're going to be just fine. You hear me?"

When she didn't respond, he lifted her chin up to his face. And that look in her eyes, of adject worry, startled him. "Oh baby," he said. "You're the most important person in this world to me. Don't you forget that."

Hood attempted to smile, although it came off as just more worry. But she managed to nod her head. "I won't," she said.

Max continued to stare into her eyes. She was so vulnerable, despite the tough exterior she presented. He could just feel her vulnerability. So much so that he leaned down and kissed her on the lips. It wasn't meant to be a passion play, and it wasn't. It was meant to remind her that he had her back and always would. "We're okay," he said to her when they stopped kissing.

Although she made another attempt at smiling, and laid her head, once again, on his chest, she knew that didn't solve anything. Because the fact still remained: what about his kid sister?

CHAPTER TWENTY-TWO

Early that next morning, Hood woke up only to find Max had gone. She also discovered that he had somehow managed to put one of his dress shirts on her and put her to bed without her even remembering any of it. Last thing she remembered was dozing off in his arms as he dozed off too.

She picked up her phone on the nightstand. It was four a.m. and he was already up? He hardly got any sleep!

She threw the covers off of her, got out of bed, and made her way to the ensuite bathroom. She felt so depressed she didn't know what she was going to do. How could she not fully support a man who basically brought her up out of the mud and sat her in his palace? And not as his side piece or his girlfriend, but as his wife? He'd been nothing but good to her. And all he did for her siblings too?

And even after she showered and brushed, and then dressed into a pair of jeans and a Bears jersey, she was still thinking about what Max had told her. How could he not go full throttle to get his sister back? How could she hold him back from that? What kind of wife would she be if she didn't do all she could to help him too?

But she wouldn't be his wife anymore if the only way to secure his sister was by divorcing her. That was the part that stung. Because she knew one thing for sure: if that woman was telling the truth and his sister was still alive, if something were to happen to the sister because of Max's refusal to divorce Hood, he would hate Hood forever. And with a bitter hate. She was convinced of that.

She put her thick, wavy hair into a ponytail and went downstairs. She heard voices as she walked down the staircase.

When she walked into the living room, Max and Jason, along with Max's chief of security Dale Perry, were seated. Max and Jason were on the sofa, while Dale sat in one of the high-back chairs. Max was seated back, his legs folded, as he read something on his iPad. Dale and Jason were small-talking. When the two men saw Hood enter the room, they quickly stood up.

"Good morning, Mrs. Cassidy," Dale said with a nod of his head. Under Max's strict order, no member of his staff was to refer to Hood as anything except Mrs. Cassidy. Even Jason did the same when others were around.

"Good morning, Dale," Hood said,

nodding back. "Hey Jason."

"Hello Mrs. Cassidy," Jason said with a smile. He always had an urge to give Hood a hug, because she reminded him so much of his own little sister, but she always looked so serious that he wasn't sure how she would receive it. She nor Max were the touchy-feely types, and he knew he had to respect that. But he did move over and let her take the seat next to Max.

When Hood sat down, she could see that Max's entire attention was buried in whatever he was reading.

She wanted to ask him what it was about, although she was pretty certain it concerned his sister or that woman or both, but she didn't say anything. She and Max still had a kind of peculiar relationship. It was as if they were still trying to feel each other out. Max could be so domineering that they often bumped heads, and Max would sometimes back down. But most times he wouldn't. If it mattered to Hood, she never backed down. Because she knew, if she gave in and gave in to a man like Max, she'd never get out of giving in.

Max finally stopped reading the report Dale had sent to him. He had been so immersed in it that he didn't realize Hood had come downstairs and was seated beside him.

And although he placed his arm around her waist, and leaned her warm, fresh-scented body against him, he was looking at Dale. "But nobody has eyeballed her outside of that video I saw?"

"That's correct, sir," said Dale. "The only thing we know for certain, as I stated in that report, is that Breena Novak does have a connection to several shady figures, but a mobster in Jersey seems to be the one most likely to have some intel for us. He seems to be one of her favorite people. We figure he either knows something about your sister, or he could tell us more about Breena that could lead us to your sister. But so far that's the only big takeaway we were able to come up with."

"And you've got every one of those men I've had on retainer for years on this too?"

"Every one of them, and every one of our people," said Dale. "But those guys on retainer are basically useless, if I'm to be honest. They're old school. But this isn't an old school case. Breena Novak isn't playing any low-level games they're used to. She knows what she's doing. We just don't know what she's doing yet."

"Who all knows about her connection to this mobster?" asked Max. "To this," Max looked at the report on his iPad, "Francis "the Monk" Paletti?"

"Nobody knows," said Dale, "except for the guys who uncovered it and those of us that are in this room."

"And nobody's approached him yet?"

"Nobody, sir. I wanted you to make that call."

Max nodded. "Then I need to go see him."

When Jason and Dale glanced at each other as if they were surprised, Hood knew it was a bad idea. Dale was looking at Jason to tell Max so.

"But Max," Jason said in his easygoing way, "are you sure you want to approach this guy? We're talking about the mob here. And he's no run-of-the-mill either. This Monk Paletti is near the top of the food chain."

Max frowned. "You think I give a fuck about his position on some mob food chain? I'm talking about my sister! If Jen's alive, I need to know it. And if this mobster, if this Monk Paletti is somebody who knows something, then I'm going to eyeball him for myself."

"Then at least let us arrange a meeting," said Jason.

But Max was shaking his head. "No way. You hip him to my interest, and he's suddenly unavailable. But if I show up to one of his hangouts while he's there, he just might be caught off-guard enough that he'll tell me something. Especially if he's as sanctimonious as you guys claim he is."

"Oh he's a cut above most mob bosses, that's for sure," said Dale. "But he's vicious too. He's married to Mick Sinatra's niece for crying out loud. He's the head of the Bonaducci crime family, and that's no easy organization to head. He doesn't do a lot of the shit most mob bosses do, but don't underestimate him. He's vicious as they come."

Hood looked at Max. "Who's Mick Sinatra?" she asked.

"A mob boss," Max said to her.

"He's the boss of all bosses," Dale said to her. "He's the top guy no question about it. Which means Monk Paletti has a lot of weight behind him. We have to be very careful, Boss."

"Oh I'll be careful. I been around guys like him all my life. Even my old man had his gangster ways. I know my way around the park."

But the idea of Max leaving again when he just got back wasn't something Hood appreciated. But she appreciated his mission. Had it been one of her siblings in that same situation, she'd be leaving on that jet plane too.

"When do you want to go?" Dale asked Max.

"What do you mean when? Today. I want to be there around noon, and it's what? A couple hours' flight? Little more? I want to be in the air by ten this morning."

"I'll arrange it," said Dale. Then he exhaled. "But there's this other matter, sir."

Max and Hood looked at Dale. "What other matter?" Max asked.

Dale looked to Jason to answer him.

"Breena's demand."

Max and Hood immediately knew what other matter they were talking about when Jason said *Breena* and *demand* in the same sentence.

"There's got to be another way," said Max.

"And if there isn't, Max?" asked Jason because they all needed to know how far down that rabbit hole Max was willing to go to get Jenny back.

But Max only repeated himself. "There has to be another way," he said. "Find it."

Dale looked at Jason. "How can they find an answer," Jason responded, "when the demand came from a woman they have no control over whatsoever, Max? How is that even possible?"

"That's the other thing," said Max. "I want you guys to get her and take her to one of our undisclosed locations."

Even Hood knew that was a bad idea. "But Max," she said, "didn't she make it clear to you that if you try anything like that you'll never see your sister again?"

"I know what she said to me. But what the fuck else am I supposed to do? What if she disappears again the way she did before? What if she dangles that carrot and take off? What am I supposed to do then? Know that my sister is out there somewhere and I spend another twenty years looking for him?"

"We have our best surveillance people on her, sir," said Dale. "There's no need to risk picking her up. There's no way she can disappear on us. That's a guarantee. But . . ."

"But what?" asked Max.

"That doesn't negate the fact, sir," said Dale, "that you've got to seriously consider her demand. Even if you just marry her long enough to get your sister back."

Max frowned. "Are you nuts? You think she's that stupid? She knows that'll be the plan. That's why it'll be a year of marriage and then I get my sister back, or some other outrageousness. Because she knows if we're together for a full year, it could . . ."

Max stopped himself. But Hood and Jason and even Dale were waiting anxiously for him to continue. Because Hood and Jason had a darn good idea what he would say if he continued. That if he stayed with Breena for a full year, that it could develop into love again? That he might not want to lose her again?

Hood's heart dropped. Because that was her greatest fear: that Max actually had feelings for the woman.

Jason's heart dropped too, because he realized something he had been overlooking all along: the love factor. That Max might still have deep feelings for Breena that he hadn't been able to shake. He hired men to search the world over for her when she ghosted him a decade ago. Why would he have done all that if he didn't have some serious feelings for her?

But Max wasn't giving an inch. "There has to be another way. Find it," was all he'd say about it.

Dale and Jason both knew Max well enough to know that there was no changing his mind when his mind was that narrowly focused.

Dale stood up. "I'll arrange your transport to New Jersey, sir," he said. "And we'll get extra security on Mrs. Cassidy while you're away," he added.

"That won't be necessary."

Everybody looked at Max. "Excuse me?" Dale asked him.

"You aren't getting any extra anything on my wife. She's going with me."

Hood, like Jason and Dale, were shocked. They all stared at Max.

"You're taking her with you?" Jason asked.

"Yes. Nobody can protect her better than I can. She's going with me."

"But you're going to meet a mob boss, Max. You can't put Hood in that kind of situation."

"Don't you tell me what I can or can't do with my own wife. And I'm not putting her in any situation. I'm keeping her with me. I'm keeping her safe."

"With respect, Max," said Jason, who was totally against it, "you didn't keep her safe that night in Utah."

Hood couldn't believe Jason went there. That night, when both Max and Hood were nearly killed, was a night to forget, not to remember. But Jason wasn't just Max's operations chief. He was Max's longtime best friend. And he didn't pacify his friend.

And Max, to Dale's surprise, seemed to take that truth in stride. "That was unexpected. This won't be. I barely knew her then. She's my wife now. There's no comparison. Now go do your jobs and get me more information than this thin bullshit you just gave me. I need more! Get on it."

"Yes, sir," Dale said and began to hurry out of the line of fire.

Jason exhaled, stood up, and grabbed up his briefcase. "I'll see you guys at the airfield."

Max and Hood looked at him. "What do you mean?" asked Max.

"I knew Jenny too. I took a leave of absence from law school to help search for her. Remember? I want her home too."

Max's heart swelled with emotion for Jason. He'd been by Max's side through thick and thin. A true best friend. But more bodies wouldn't help. "I need you to stay here," he said, "in case we get any new intel on Breena."

Jason didn't like it, but he understood it. And he left.

Hood looked at Max. "Thanks," she said. "For what?"

"Taking me with you."

"That's an easy call for me. Nobody can protect you better than I can."

Hood smiled. "I can protect myself and you too. I'm the one who saved your ass from that carjacker in Utah, remember?"

"I was going to handle him myself, I keep telling you that."

"Sure Max," said Hood and they looked

at each other and smiled. But then Max thought about what they were truly up against, and how he had so much to lose between his sister and his wife, that a heavy feeling of dread came over him. A feeling he didn't want, couldn't shoulder, and needed to get rid of. And the only human being on earth that could help him do that was sitting right beside him.

And Hood knew it too. She knew that look Max was giving to her. And that was why, when he stood up and reached out his hand to her, she didn't hesitate. She stood up, too, and then they walked, hand in hand, up that staircase.

CHAPTER TWENTY-THREE

Riding. That was what it felt like whenever Max was inside of her. Like a comfortable, thick and creamy, smooth ride.

But not this time. Max wasn't his usual smooth-operator self. He was his *in need* self. And whenever he was in need, there was nothing smooth about it.

He was pounding her hard as he did her. They had both stripped naked, they were both in the center of their bed, and he was going for it. He was taking them there. And as he pumped and groaned and pumped and groaned, Hood held onto him, wrapping her legs around his body, and gave him full access.

And Max took full advantage of that access. He loved when she understood. He loved that she knew this was more about releasing tension and stress and pain than it was about making each other feel good. He needed to feel better. That was the difference. He needed to feel as if it was going to be alright and he would get his sister home.

And Hood was making it happen for him. He pumped her and sucked her breasts so hard and kissed her so passionately that even she was groaning too. Even she was in the throes of their passion too.

And when he came, which didn't take nearly as long as it usually did for them, she came too. Neither one of them could hold out any longer. And although their lovemaking was rough, their cum was as intense as it always was. They came hard too.

And then Max, well spent, rolled off of Hood and then pulled her on top of him. But even Hood knew their coupling only helped in that moment. Because Max was already thinking about the situation again.

Hood looked at him and rubbed his hair. He looked downright distressed. "We'll find her, Max."

"I believe that too."

And then they just laid there, arm in arm, until they fell asleep.

Two hours later and Hood was awake again. She lifted her head and looked at Max. He was snoring hard and fast asleep. Which she knew was a good thing for him. He needed the sleep. But she couldn't do it.

She grabbed her phone, eased off of Max's naked body, went down the hall into one of their guestroom bathrooms. And as soon as she closed the door, she began to sob. They hadn't been married two months and all of this was already on their plate? And how selfish was she to want it all to just go away? But that was what she wanted. God help her, that was what she was praying for.

She looked at her phone. It was just after seven am. And with no one else to call, she called her big sister. But it didn't take long for Rita to know she wasn't just calling her to shoot the breeze. Not that time of morning. And the little Hood did tell Rita, she swore her to secrecy.

But after Hood hung up the phone, she thought that was the end of her venting. But she had only to dress back into her jeans and jersey and get downstairs to make herself a cup of coffee before Rita, still in her pants pajamas and an overcoat, was already at her front door.

"What do you mean he has to divorce you?" she asked bewilderedly as soon as Hood opened the door.

CHAPTER TWENTY-FOUR

"Where is he anyway?" Rita sat at the center island.

Hood was standing at the island preparing coffee. "Still asleep."

"But what do you mean he has to divorce you?"

"Rita, I told you this is between you and me."

"And that's why I'm asking you."

"You can't tell anybody about this. Especially not Max. And not even Ricky either."

"Okay. Dang! What's the big deal?"

"The big deal is that what I'm telling you is extremely private, Rita. That's what's the big deal." Then a distressed look appeared on Hood's face. "I just need somebody to talk to about it, that's all. I don't know what to do."

Rita looked at her kid sister. She was so far over her head it wasn't even funny. That was why she wanted them to do their own thing. They were all too dependent on Max. Especially Hood. When Rita had a sinking feeling that Max couldn't be all he presented himself to be. He was too rich, too arrogant, and too domineering. But she couldn't tell Hood that. She so wanted her marriage to work that she wasn't thinking straight. "Have you tried to talk to Max about it?" she asked her.

"How can I talk to Max when it's about Max?" A look of anguish appeared in Hood's big eyes. "He's not looking at it clearly either. He can't see the forest for the trees. And in a way, neither can I. He just found out that his sister might still be alive yesterday. He's still trying to process it all."

"But where is this woman?"

"She's still in New York. He's got people on her. He's supposed to let her know something by tomorrow."

"And what is it he's going to let her know? Whether he's going to divorce you? I don't get what that has to do with his sister. What's that all about?"

"That's the condition she put on him if he wants to ever see his sister again. He has to divorce me and marry her. That's what she's saying he has to do, and then he'll get his sister back."

"Why don't he just go to the FBI, Hood? They'll make her produce that so-called sister of Max's."

But Hood was shaking her head. "If he did anything like that, he'll never see his sister again. She promised him that. And he seems to believe her."

"His former lover he believes," said Rita with snark in her voice. "And what about this sister? Nobody never even heard of this sister before. In everything I read about Maxwell Cassidy there's no article anywhere that brings up any kidnapped sister."

"He keeps a very low profile, Rita, I told you that." She handed Rita a cup of coffee. "His family never went to the press about this"

"Yeah, I hear what you're saying. But I don't know, Hood. You sure this sister even exists?"

Hood was about to sip her own cup of coffee when Rita made that accusation. She stopped just as the cup touched her lips. And she sat the cup down. And frowned. "Why on earth would Max lie about something like that? Why on earth would you even think something like that?"

"You said she was his ex-lover, right?"

"So?"

"Which means, if my math is correct, the man was cheating on his wife to be with this lover. Right?"

"Wrong. He didn't cheat on his wife."

"He says."

"What's your point, Reet?" Hood had irritation in her voice.

"My point is you don't know what this man is capable of. That's my point! You didn't know him all that long before y'all got married, and y'all haven't been married two months yet. And now suddenly some woman appears out of the blue? A woman he used to be fucking around with?" Rita shook her head. "Something ain't right here, Hood. I'm sorry. This shit stank."

Hood already had her doubts about everything too, but she didn't believe for a second that Max fabricated a sister and an ex-lover's return just to divorce her or whatever Rita was insinuating. Max didn't roll like that.

"If it's all about divorcing me," Hood said to her sister, "he could do that any day of the week. He wouldn't have to make up lies. He'd just do it."

"Men can be cowards when it comes to something like divorce," said Rita.

Hood wanted to ask Rita how would she

know, since she'd never been married, but she didn't go there. Rita meant well. She was a mama bear when it came to Hood, and Hood knew it. "He's not lying about this, okay? I'm sorry I even told you if you're gonna come with all that negative shit."

Rita stared at her proud, super-stubborn sister. "Why did you tell me about it if it's no big deal to you?"

"I didn't say it wasn't a big deal. It is a big deal, are you joking? It's consuming my life. But none of my distress involves Max lying to me or cheating on me. That's not my energy. That's yours."

"Okay. Let me put it another way," said Rita. "When that woman came to him with this demand that he divorce you and marry her, what did he tell her? Did he say hell no, I'll never divorce my wife? Did he tell her that?"

Hood didn't respond.

"That would be a no," said Rita. Then Rita frowned. "Hood, how could he? That man is actually considering divorcing you to marry his side piece? And you haven't thrown him out of the house yet?"

"His sister's life is at stake! Don't you understand that?"

"So he says," said a still-doubtful Rita.

But Hood shook her head. That was why

she and females rarely got along. She could never reason with them! They reach a conclusion based on little or no information, and they take off running with it. And Rita was the queen of the run. Why oh why, she wondered, did she tell her sister about any of it? "I'm done with this conversation," she said.

"But I'm not done with it," said Rita. "You need to know the truth. You need to know why he didn't tell her that."

"I thought I heard voices."

Hood and Rita both looked over and saw Max walk into the kitchen. He wore only a pair of pants, but no shirt. And every time Rita saw him, she became even more doubtful that a man that fine could be faithful to her kid sister, or to anybody for that matter. And that new information Hood had just laid on her only fed her suspicious mind.

"Why didn't he tell who?" Max asked. "And who is he?"

Hood was relieved that Max apparently only heard the tail end of their conversation. But she was shocked when Rita decided to tell him what she meant.

"I was just asking my sister if you told that woman hell no when she said you had to divorce your wife and marry her."

Hood looked at her sister as if she was

seeing her for the first time. She told her in ten different ways that their conversation had to remain private and between the two of them only. Now she was telling Max? The main person she told her she couldn't tell? Hood was floored!

But Max was irritated. Less at Rita, but mainly at Hood. He looked at her. "I didn't give you permission to discuss my business with anybody," he said.

Rita was offended. "You didn't give her *permission*?"

Hood ignored Rita. "I had to talk to somebody," she said to Max.

"Then you talk to me!" he fired back.

"Somebody other than you," Hood said. Then she frowned. "And you don't tell me who to talk to. This isn't just your business, Max. It's mine too."

"I'm saying," Rita said.

Max gave Rita a hard look.

"You still didn't answer my question," said Rita, looking just as hard right back at him. "Why didn't you tell the bitch hell no?"

"None of your fucking business. How about that?"

Rita didn't expect him to come back at her that hard. It threw her for a minute because she suddenly remembered the man wasn't just her sister-in-law. He was her boss.

Hood didn't expect him to go that hard at her sister either. She looked at Max too.

Max didn't mean to be nasty because he really liked Rita, but he was struggling with that very issue himself and he didn't need anybody from the cheap seats trying to tell him what they thing he should or shouldn't be doing. That shit bothered him.

But Rita didn't care. She regained her courage and pounced away. "I just don't think you should let anybody dangle your marriage out there like that," she said.

"And I should care what you think why?"

The way he said it, like so many men had spoken to her before, and something broke within Rita. So much so that she grabbed her cup of coffee and threw it at Max, just missing him. "Because I'm your wife's sister, you bastard!" she yelled at him. "That's why!"

"Rita!" Hood was stunned when she saw that hot coffee flying.

And Max, who deftly avoided any contact with the flying liquid, gave Rita an even angrier look. "Get the fuck out of my house," he ordered her. "Get out!"

But Hood looked at him. "Oh hell no," she said angrily. "You aren't kicking my sister out of this house. I invited her over to talk with her.

You're the one who talked to her like she was nothing, which I won't have, Max. She might be your employee, and you're used to talking to your employees any kind of way, but she's my sister first. And you won't talk to her like that. I would have thrown coffee on your ass too, if it was me."

Rita always knew her sister was tough, but she thought Max had softened her. She thought wrong. She looked at Max. She could tell he was pissed.

He looked at Hood. "Get her out of this house," he said firmly, though not angrily the way he had been responding to Rita, and then he glanced at Rita and left the kitchen.

Hood looked at Rita. Rita began rising from her seat. "I'm leaving," she said.

"You don't have to go," said Hood.

"Oh I'm going alright. He can keep his precious house," she added as Hood reluctantly walked her out to her car.

When they got to the car, they looked at one another. "He's a bastard, Hood. You can't trust him."

"Based on what evidence, Rita? Because he's rich?"

"Yes! And he's great looking. Guys like that don't ever do right. He's a bastard."

"A bastard who found you and Tim and

Ricky. A bastard who gave y'all jobs and bought y'all very nice houses to live in. Who took me out of nothing and made me his wife. But he's a bastard because he doesn't appreciate you telling him what he should or shouldn't do about his own life, and in his own house?"

"I can talk! He's not gonna stop me from talking."

"I told you not to mention anything we discussed with Max or anybody else. I told you that, Rita. But you did it anyway. How did you expect him to react?"

Rita knew she was out of line. But guys like Max always stepped over people like her, and she was tired of it.

Hood sensed more was at work with Rita, too, than what they were discussing. She stared at her sister. "Didn't go so well with the guy you went home with last night?" she asked her.

A depressed look appeared in Rita's eyes. "It went as expected. He didn't take me home with him. He took me to some seedy motel, got what he wanted, and then gave me money to call an Uber. Didn't even want me to leave with him. But I'm used to that too."

Hood's heart dropped. "But you don't have to be used to that, Rita. Get un-used to it. Stop letting guys do that to you."

"And then do what? Become Mother

Teresa like you were and wait for some arrogant billionaire to sweep me off my feet too? Girl bye! You don't know the half of it, Hood."

Then Rita stared at her sister. "Thanks for standing up for me in there," she said.

Hood didn't respond. She never liked going against Max, but she'd do it all day long if it was called for.

"What are you gonna do?" Rita asked her.

"We're going to New Jersey to talk to somebody who may know something about Jennifer."

"That's the sister's name?"

Hood nodded. "Yep."

"So Max is trying to avoid the question."

"He just wants his sister back, Rita. And he's going about it the best way he knows how. That's all he's doing. And I'm going to be right there by his side."

"And if he breaks your heart the way I'm sure he broke his first wife's heart? What then, Hood?"

But Hood was shaking her head. "Max wouldn't do that to me."

"That's what every female says before their husbands leave them. What then, Hood?" she asked again.

"Then I'll live. That's what then. I'll do

what I need to do. I survived before Max, and I'll survive after Max."

"Can I ask you something personal?"

Hood smiled. "Now you ask permission? What is it, Reet?"

"Did he make you sign a prenuptial agreement?"

Hood couldn't believe she went there. "Why did I ever involve you in my personal business?" But she answered her question to put a period on that train of thought. "No, Rita, he did not ask me to sign any prenup, nor did I sign one. Okay?"

Rita exhaled. And actually smiled. "Okay."

Hood hugged her sister with a long embrace, said her goodbyes, and then began walking back toward the entrance.

Rita watched her kid sister leave, and a part of her was jealous of Hood. She was always jealous of Hood. Even when Hood was little, she was the one who would stand up to bullies and bad people, including their mother. She was the one who was run out of town based on lies, but managed make herself a decent living in Utah. She was the one who caught the eye of a billionaire who didn't use her and abuse her and spit her out, but actually married her and brought her to his castle. Hood always landed on her feet. Rita landed too, but always in the bushes or the hedges or the river where she couldn't swim and had to figure it all out by her lonesome. She didn't hate Max. Because Hood was right that he'd done a lot for them. She hated that she never had a man to treat her like a lady the way Max treated Hood. It was her lot in life she hated.

But what was the point in obsessing over something she didn't see how she could change?

She got in her car, and took off.

CHAPTER TWENTY-FIVE

Max was lying on their bed re-reading that report on his iPad when Hood walked into the room. Max didn't bother to look up as she plopped on the other side of the bed and sat, Indian-style, at his side.

"She's gone?" Max asked without looking away from the report.

"Yes."

"Don't you ever discuss what goes on in this household with her or anybody else again," he said. Then he looked at Hood. "Do you understand me?"

Hood agreed that what she'd done wasn't helpful at all. It only put him and Rita in the crossfire. "Yes," she said.

"If you need somebody to talk to you talk to me when it concerns our business. Nothing good will come when you put your business in the street. And you know how private I try to live my life."

Hood understood, he could see it in her sad, expressive eyes. "I'm sorry," she said. "I shouldn't have told Rita what I told her. But she meant well. She was only looking out for me. But I shouldn't have said anything."

That was why Max loved Hood so completely. She owned her shit better than any human being alive. And she called him out on his too. "I was out of line the way I spoke to your sister. She was right to be angry with me. I'll apologize to her."

Hood looked at Max and smiled. Then she moved over to him and laid beside him, wrapping her arms around his bare chest. She also looked at that report on his iPad. "Still reviewing it?"

"I just want to make sure I'm not missing something. It feels like I'm missing something."

"Have you considered the alternative," Hood decided to ask him.

He looked at her. "What alternative?"

"What if this woman, this Breena, was telling you a pack of lies? What if she's running game on you in such a way that we can't even conceive of? She had to know that the long lost sister of a billionaire is worth gold to anybody with any information about her. You'd give a fortune to get your sister back. She has to know that."

Max nodded. "Yeah, I thought about that too."

"And I'm sure she knew how you felt about your sister. You were dating her when she was taken, wasn't you? She was there when she was kidnapped," Hood said. "Wasn't she?"

But when she said it, Max's entire expression changed.

"What is it?" Hood asked him. "What's wrong?"

He sat straight up on the bed.

"What is it, Max?" Hood, now on her elbows, was now anxious to know what it was she said that struck such a nerve with him.

"She was there," Max said. "She was the person I was upstairs with when Jen was taken."

Hood was shocked. She didn't mention who the girl was upstairs with him when he told her the story. "She was in the house when your sister was kidnapped?"

Max nodded, but his mind seemed to be ahead of that. "Yes."

"But what does that mean?"

Max looked at Hood. "She didn't look for her."

That surprised Hood. "She didn't?"

"We had search parties everywhere, and everybody we knew were searching for my sister. But I remember being surprised that Breena wasn't joining in on any searches. And whenever I wanted to talk to her about it, she'd claim it was too depressing to talk about and change the subject."

"*Change the subject*?" That was odd even to Hood.

"And then she just wasn't around anymore. For months on end. She disappeared too."

Max and Hood looked at each other, and then Max sat his iPad aside and began getting out of bed.

"What are you doing? It's five in the morning. We aren't leaving until ten."

"I need to see Breena," Max said as he began putting back on his clothes. "She's going to cut the bullshit with me and tell me all she knows."

"Or?"

"Or I'll beat it out of her ass."

"Or?"

Max stared at Hood. "Or you don't wanna know."

But Hood was shaking her head. "You can't, Max. I know how you feel, but you can't. You said we can't do that or it could jeopardize your sister. She's wired, remember? Max?"

But Hood could tell he wasn't listening to her anymore. He was in his own world now. And she hopped out of bed quickly and began dressing too. No way was he going on his own. No way was she letting him ruin all hope of getting his sister back just because he was angry at some bitch who never should have come at him the way she did.

But Max wasn't waiting around. He dressed quickly and was heading downstairs. All he could think about was getting to Breena and doing everything in his power to get her to tell him everything she knew. And not just what was behind that *divorce your wife and marry me* nonsense either. Because he wasn't agreeing to do shit until he found out everything she knew about his sister, and where she was, and what she knew seventeen years ago too. No more bullshit. No more leaving it to others to do his dirty work. He wanted answers now.

Max left the room so fast that Hood had no choice but to grab her shoes and run. She hurried down those stairs behind him.

But Max wasn't hurrying to his car. He was in his downstairs office, opening up his massive, wall-sized gun cabinet, when Hood hurried in. She sat on his desk and put on her tennis shoes as she watched him pull out the big gun.

"Get one for me too," she said.

CHAPTER TWENTY-SIX

Max's private plane arrived in New York city around seven that morning. An SUV met them at the airfield and transported them straight to the Merrimount hotel, where they made their way to the top floor.

The elevator doors opened and as soon as Max and Hood stepped out, they were accosted by Breena's security team that asked if they could frisk them.

But Max looked at them as if they'd grown wings. "What the fuck do you need to frisk us for? She approached me, I didn't approach her. She asked me a question and I'm coming to answer it. Hell no you aren't frisking me, and you sure as hell not frisking my wife. And if that's a problem, my ass can leave."

The men looked at each other as if they weren't sure what to do. Then they stepped aside.

But once they cleared that security hurdle, another security team was waiting for them at the door of the suite.

Which confused Hood. She leaned against Max and whispered to him. "Why would she have more security than you do if she's just the messenger they don't care about?" she asked him.

"That's what I'm wondering too," Max responded. But he was also wondering if he had just walked into a trap, and had taken Hood right along with him!

When they got up to the door of the suite, the guard at the door stopped them there too. "Just a moment, sir." Then the guard knocked on the door and waited for a response.

When Max heard woman's voice yell *enter*, and the guard walked in and closed the door behind him, he exhaled. Hood noticed the change in him. "That her voice?" she asked him.

Max nodded. "Yup."

But even Hood could tell just her voice alone did something to Max. Was it just the stress of what her presence meant back in his life? Or did he still had feelings for this girl? Could that be it? Hood was dying to see her.

The guard opened the door wide for Max and Hood to walk on in. Then he stepped out and closed them inside of the suite.

At first, nobody was present. Just your standard luxurious hotel suite. Then they heard that voice again.

"Max, darling," she said, and Max and Hood looked up at the top of the staircase. "You're early."

And there she was. The woman Max called Breena Novak. Hood was astounded by her beauty.

Max was astounded by her beauty, too, as she walked down the stairs. She wore a gown, a gorgeous white gown that hugged all her curves, and that fit her like a second skin. Hood immediately knew she was out of this woman's league. There was no comparison! She looked at Max. By the way he was looking at Breena, he seemed to realize it too.

"I expected you to take the full two days," Breena said as she walked up to them. "Based on our conversation on yesterday, I fully expected it." But her entire focus was on Hood. "This must be your Hood? Isn't that her name?"

"Yes," Max said as if the spell was suddenly broken. "This is my wife."

Breena didn't look Hood up and down because she knew Max. It was always a face thing for Max. What was in that face? And Breena saw right away why Max would have chosen to marry this one. Breena could see that Hood had that rarest of combinations in her face alone: a streetwise toughness, and a staggering innocence too. It was a remarkable face. And for the first time Breena's confidence began to take a small hit. It was one thing to see a photograph of someone and declare no competition. It was something entirely different to see that competition in person. And standing beside Max. And Max placing his hand around her waist just because Breena called her by her actual name. But, as Max accurately picked up on, she was calling her that name maliciously. "Have a seat," she said to them.

Max and Hood sat on the sofa. Breena sat in the chair and crossed her legs in such a way that the split in the gown nearly revealed too much. But Hood was certain it was meant to.

Breena smiled, still staring at Hood. "I don't mean to stare," she said, "but you look so much younger than Max. How old are you exactly?"

Max gave Breena a hard look. He knew she was going for the jugular.

But Hood knew it too. "How old are you?" Hood asked.

Breena smiled. "You're a quick one. I like that! But honey let's put it this way."

"That's enough, Breena," Max warned.

"I'm answering her question. Do you wish for me to answer your question?" Breena asked Hood.

Hood knew it was a trap of her own making, but she nodded her head. "Yes," she said.

"You're young," said Breena. "I'm legendary. That's how old I am."

"That old, hun?" Hood fired back. "I thought legends were retirees."

Max raised his eyebrows in pleasant surprise that Hood could hold her own even against an old pro like Bree. But Hood wasn't nearly as confident as her face would suggest. She could easily see why Max would want to marry a woman like Breena. She'd fit right into his world. There would be no learning curve whatsoever. There would be no need to show her any ropes. Hood was worried.

Breena was worried, too, because she wasn't accustomed to real competition. And that slip of a girl was the real deal. Even Breena saw that. She was not going to intimidate that one, that was for damn sure.

Breena sat upright and hugged her knees with her hands. "The reason you're here I take it," she said to Max, "is to give me your decision."

"I'm not divorcing my wife," said Max, "if that's the decision you mean."

But Hood knew they couldn't be rash about something this serious. "Max," she said before he went too far.

But in Breena's mind, he'd already gone too far. "You do realize what that means, right? You do realize that it was your negligence that caused Jenny to be kidnapped in the first place, and that what you just said to me will ensure that you'll kill her again? That you'll seal her fate forever when you're so close to a reunion?"

That comment reminded Hood how dire their situation was. But Max was angry. "You won't lay that shit at my feet," he said to Breena. "I have no demands on the table. I just want to see my sister again. I just want to see that she's okay."

"I gave you proof of life. The only thing left is your agreement to the deal. You don't agree and you'll never see her again because there won't be any *her* to see."

"Bullshit!" Max yelled.

"Max," said Hood, worried that he was letting his considerable temper get in the way of his reasoning.

But Max knew what he was doing. He knew how to handle Breena.

"Bullshit?" Breena asked.

"That's what I said."

"You think what we're doing is bullshit?" Then she smiled a smile that made her even more attractive. "You are the gambler, aren't you, Max? Always has been. That's why you're so successful. You take risks others won't take. But guess what? You're gambling with Jenny's life once again."

"You were there when they kidnapped her," Max said, catching her off guard.

Breena stared at Max. "So? We were fooling around then. So what?"

"Why didn't you help me find her? You eased out of my life then. I didn't see you for months."

"You were obsessed with finding your sister, and rightfully so. I didn't want to stand in your way."

But Max and Hood were staring at her.

"That has nothing to do with this," Breena said, suddenly defensive. "I need to know your final decision. Are you going to agree to terms or not? Are you going to kill that child again, Max, or not?"

"I'm not divorcing my wife!" Max yelled. "Those are my terms."

"Max," said Hood.

"Come up with new terms and then we'll talk," Max added.

"Max, I need to talk to you," said Hood. "Can we talk?"

"Yes," said Breena. "I would strongly advise a conversation before Jenny's fate is sealed."

Max gave Breena an angry glare. But then he looked at Hood. And he could see the anxiousness in her eyes. "I'm not divorcing you.

I'm not going along with any nonsense she cooks up."

"Go out in the hall and discuss it," said Breena. "Your wife, I'm sure, will give you a clearer picture of what your decision means. Your wife, I'm sure, will help get you off of that deadly position. Got talk privately. Or you'll regret it later."

"Fuck you, Breena."

Breena stood up and removed her entire gown off of her body, revealing a body completely naked except for the wires and microphone strapped around her waist. "Go outside, Max, and talk this over."

Seeing those wires reminded Max what he was up against. He already knew whomever had Jen could hear their conversations. They heard them in that boardroom when Breena became afraid of Max's anger and they quickly showed him that proof of life video. He got up, took Hood's hand, and they left the room.

But Hood looked back at Breena. "Give us a moment," she said.

"That would be wise," said Breena.

Hood gave Breena a hard glare too, because she was smiling so smugly as she stood there naked with her perfect body, but Hood knew she was right about one thing. Max was being far too rash, and too unyielding, at the worst possible time. They left the room.

In the hall they moved out of earshot of the guards at the door. But Max's mind was made up. "I'm not giving in to that shit she's talking about, Hood. It's a trap, I can feel it's a trap. I'm not divorcing you."

"But what about your sister?"

"I'm not divorcing you."

"But if it'll get your sister back, don't you think we need to consider that? I hate saying it. I don't want that either, you know I don't. But we have to think about Jen."

Max ran his hands through his hair. He hated the position Breena's demand had put him in.

Hood hated that she had to be the voice of reason. But somebody had to be. "Even if you did have to divorce me," she threw out there, "it'll only be temporary. It'll only be until you reconnect with your sister."

But Max was shaking her head. "It doesn't work like that, Hood. We're talking people, not process. If I divorce you, even temporarily, that means I put somebody else ahead of you. You'll never trust me with your heart ever again, I don't care what you say. We'll never be the same again."

"And if you lose Jen again? We'll never be the same if that happens."

But Max knew it wouldn't work. Something was off. "I'm not taking that risk," he said. "These people are up to something. I'm not taking that risk."

"Not even for your sister?"

It was a bitter pill for Max to swallow, but it was the truth. "Not even for Jenny," he said.

But Hood continued to stare at him. She wasn't buying it. "Is it my reaction to your decision you're worried about," she asked, "or your reaction to Breena if she becomes your wife?"

Max frowned. "What's that supposed to mean?"

"Are you worried that you'll fall in love with her again, and may not be so quick to want to lose her again?"

Hood had expected Max to object with fire in his nostrils. But the fact that he hesitated and said nothing right away, said it all to Hood.

"No," Max finally said. "That's not it."

But if he sounded convincing to himself, he sounded quite the opposite to Hood.

And Max, feeling exposed, pulled Hood into his arms. "It's you I want. Nobody else," he said with a frown on his face.

"But you're afraid," said Hood as she pulled back from him to get a look at his eyes, "that once you have her again, you'll want her too."

Max shook his head. "No," he said. "No way."

But his eyes said *yes way*. And the eyes, in Hood's mind, always had it.

But she felt it was her job to protect Max, even from himself, and no matter the consequences for herself. "You need to think about your sister," she said, "more than about me or yourself or anybody else. She showed you the proof of life. Your sister's out there. You'll never forgive yourself or me or anybody else if she ends up dead because you didn't move everything to save her."

Max knew it too. But why did Hood have to be the sacrifice? Why couldn't it be him? Why was the world always beating up on Hood?

"I'll go back in," he said, "and tell her I want to take that extra day I still have. I'll tell her my decision tomorrow."

"And what will that do, Max?"

"That'll give us some time to go see that mobster and see what he knows. That'll buy me some time."

It was pure desperation and Hood knew it. But she went along with it. It was better than him giving Breena that hard no he was ready to give to her.

It was also playing with fire and Hood

228

knew that too. But she knew how much Max loved her. And even if they had to be apart for a little while, she couldn't believe he'd leave her for somebody else. He loved her. She was depending on that love to see them through.

But Max was still torn. It was painful for him in every sense of the word. But he knew Hood was right. It would kill him if he blew the one chance he had in seventeen years to get Jenny back. He wasn't sacrificing Hood to do it. But he knew something had to give.

"Ready?" Max said to Hood.

"Are you ready is the question," Hood said to Max.

And Max nodded. As ready as he would ever be, he supposed. And they made their way back to the door. He still had that extra day. Buying time. That was what it was. That was what it felt like.

The guard knocked and waited for a response. When he got none, he knocked again. When there was still no response, both guards glanced at each other.

"Miss Novak?" said the guard that had knocked on the door. "Miss Novak?"

When there was still no response, Max and Hood looked at each other. She knew they were coming right back? What was with the melodrama?

The guard was asking himself that question too. He decided to open the door. "Miss Novak? Miss Novak, Mr. Cassidy wishes to see you again, ma'am. Miss Novak?"

Max, suddenly feeling anxious, moved the guard aside and looked into the room. When he saw what looked like an overturned chair, he ran into the room. Hood and the guards ran in behind him.

"Is that blood?" Hood asked as she pointed to a stain near the overturned chair.

The guard ran over to the stain and touched it. "It's blood," he said. "It's blood!"

Max and Hood nearly died where they stood.

CHAPTER TWENTY-SEVEN

But they weren't so thrown that they couldn't follow the lead guard into the room that he said was Breena's bedroom. "Miss Novak?" the guard was yelling, but this time with panic in his voice. "*Miss Novak*?"

"Was a guard on that door all night?" asked Max as they ran.

"Yes, sir. There's no way out of here except through the front door and we were guarding it the whole time. She was the only one in this suite. Nobody came."

But Breena wasn't in the bedroom either. Then they all ran into the second bedroom. But still no Breena. Then they all ran upstairs.

The lead guard was in pure panic mode. "She's not here!" he said as they looked into the only room upstairs. "How could she not be here? We were on that door all night! She was the only one in here!"

"Who do you work for?" Max asked.

"Bauch Security," said the second guard.

Max had heard of the company. "Do you know who employed Bauch for this job?"

"No, sir."

Max immediately pulled out his phone

and contacted the chief of the detail he had downstairs. "She's gone," he said as soon as the chief came on the phone. "Have you seen her?"

"No, sir."

"Alert all units to be on the lookout. She's missing."

"Yes, sir."

Then Max called Dale Perry, the chief of all of his security operations.

"Sir?"

"Phone Bauch Security. Find out who hired them to guard the penthouse suite in the Merrimount, and what was the reason given."

"Everything okay, sir?"

"No. She's gone. Breena's gone." Then he ended the call.

"Is there a connecting door in this suite?" Hood asked the guards.

"No way. It's the only suite on this floor. It's the penthouse suite!"

But Max knew a thing or two about penthouses. And he hurried to the closet upstairs and began pressing his hand against the wall. But nothing happened. Then Max grabbed Hood and ran back downstairs, with the guards following them.

Max ran into the first bedroom's closet and did the same pressing, but nothing

232

happened again. And then he ran into the second bedroom downstairs. But when he went into that closet and pressed the right side of that wall, something finally gave.

To the surprise of both guards and Hood too, the wall suddenly became a door, and it opened.

"I'll be damn!" said the first guard.

And when that door opened, there it was: a back stairwell. And there was blood on the stairs.

Max grabbed Hood and began running down those stairs.

"Where does it lead?" asked the second guard.

"The parking garage I'm sure."

"But we're forty floors up," said the first guard.

But Max was certain they stopped on one of the lower floors and took the elevator on down. Which was exactly what they did too.

But when they got down to the parking garage, it was nothing to see there. The parking attendant couldn't give them any information either. Cars were going and coming all the time, even at that time of morning. It was useless.

But Max got Dale Perry on the phone again. When he confirmed that the entity that hired Bauch Security to guard Breena utilized the company's complete anonymity option, paid up front, and left no traceable trail, Max wanted to scream. Breena was gone, there was blood in her room, and nobody, not even his own men, knew where the fuck she was? He wanted to tear somebody apart!

But then he thought about that mobster in Jersey. Because the man they called The Monk was looking less and less like the longshot he'd always been, and more and more like the only shot they had.

He took Hood's hand and hurried out of that garage.

CHAPTER TWENTY-EIGHT

Francis "the Monk" Paletti entered the old mansion like a man who'd rather be anywhere else, and was escorted to the parlor room.

Don Bonaducci, the Head Emeritus of the Bonaducci Crime Syndicate, was seated in a wheelchair with a blanket over his aching knees. Monk Paletti became his handpicked successor after Raymond Paletti, Monk's own father, faltered as head of the family. The family, under Monk, was just beginning to thrive, which The Don appreciated. But he still liked to put in his two cents to remind everybody that he wasn't dead yet.

Monk leaned down and gave him a kiss on each cheek. And then sat in the chair in front of him.

"I love ya'," Don Bonaducci said in his raspy, heavily Jersey-accented voice, "but you're late."

Monk wasn't late. He was, in fact, a few minutes early, so he didn't respond. Sometimes The Don was as lucid as a man half his age. Other times he had cobwebs.

"Where's the Misses? Why isn't she here with you? The other wives are downstairs. The men are upstairs."

"The men and their mistresses," said Monk.

"And so? What's your point, Frankie?"

"I told you how I feel about that," said Monk. "I don't like that shit. I'm not putting my wife in that shit."

"You're the head of the family now, Frankie. It don't matter what you like or don't like. It's what the men like. And they like this perk. And their wives understand they need this perk. But how does it look when everybody in the organization participates, except the leader of that organization? That don't look right, Frankie."

"Then it just won't look right. I'm not participating and I'm not having my wife around it."

But it still didn't sit right with The Don. "You treat her like she better than our wives. She ain't no better. And the fact that she ain't one of us, not even Italian, makes it imperative, Frankie, that you get her involved. Or I'm telling you there will be a revolt. And Teddy Sinatra and his old man ain't gonna get you out of this one. And I'm too old to lift a finger. Get her involved, Frankie."

Monk nodded, to move the conversation along, but there was no way Ashley was going to become a *look the other way* wife the way they did things in the family. Big Daddy Sinatra would kick his ass first of all. Then Teddy. And then Reno, Tommy, and Sal Gabrini would join in. And then Mick Sinatra would kill him. But it didn't matter. Once The Don was dead, he was ending that bullshit anyway.

"You wanted to see me about something specific?" Monk asked.

The Don leaned back in his wheelchair. "I hear you got a problem."

"Oh yeah? What problem is that?"

"A Slavitt problem."

Monk hesitated. How would The Don know about that? "How would you know about that?" asked Monk.

"I hear things."

"You hear it from whom?"

"From whom? Listen to you. I hear things, what difference does it make who from?"

Then The Don started coughing uncontrollably. Monk used to jump up to assist him, but he now knew how much The Don hated anybody assisting him whatsoever. They just had to wait it out.

Monk waited it out. The coughing waned and then ended altogether. And The Don was lucid again. "Clean that shit up, Frankie," he said. "We got enough problems. We don't need somebody else's."

And then the uncontrollable coughing resumed. But this time it wasn't going away. And his attendant entered the room and wheeled The Don into the onsite hospital. Just a matter of time, Monk knew, before The Don would no longer be with them. And right after he was put in the ground, all kinds of challenges to his authority were going to spring up. All hell was going to break out.

But until then, he was the boss. And he had work to do.

CHAPTER TWENTY-NINE

The rented SUV drove up to the diner off the highway and Max got out from behind the steering wheel and opened the front passenger door for Hood. When they walked inside, there were no customers. But there were people around.

Monk Paletti, for instance, was seated sideways at the bar, the bottom of his feet pressed against the side of a bar stool, and he was talking with the bartender. Another man, one of Monk's capos, got up when they walked in and walked over to them. Everybody in the place, except for Monk himself, appeared to be big, burly Italian guys all old enough to be Monk's father. The kind of men who'd been around the block so many times there was no telling what hell they'd seen.

"You're in the wrong place," the capo said as soon as he walked over to Max and Hood.

"If Francis Paletti's here," said Max, "I'm in the exact right place. The Monk here?"

The capo looked Max up and down. Even casually dressed, Max had an air about him that reeked of wealth. "Who's asking?" he asked.

"Maxwell Cassidy."

Even the big lug heard that name before, Hood could tell, because his bulldog expression changed. "One moment," he said, and made his way over to Monk.

Max and Hood watched as the capo waited until Monk had finished saying whatever he was saying to the bartender. When he finished and looked at the capo, the capo whispered in his ear. Monk then looked over at Max and Hood. But his expression didn't change. Monk simply got up from his stool and disappeared down a corridor beside the bar.

The capo walked back over to Max and Hood. "Follow me," he said, and the twosome did as they were told.

They, too, were escorted down the same corridor Monk had disappeared down, and then they were at a door at the end of the hall. The capo knocked once and opened it, and then opened it wide enough for Hood and then Max to walk through. The capo closed the door behind them and stood guard outside of the door.

Monk was leaned against the front of the desk, his legs folded at the ankles. He motioned for them to sit down. They sat down.

"What do I owe the pleasure?" Monk

asked.

"Where's Breena Novak?" asked Max.

There was a hesitation on Monk's part. But then he smiled. "Why would I know where she is?"

Max wasn't trying to small talk with the mobster. He got to the point. "She showed up in my life after a decade and told me she knew where my kidnapped sister was, and then she disappeared on me again."

Monk seemed surprised to hear what he'd just heard. "Who is your kidnapped sister?" he asked Max.

"Jennifer Cassidy. She was three when she was snatched. Now she'd be twenty. You know her?"

Monk nodded his head no. Max and Hood appreciated the fact that he didn't play games with them. "And you think Bree knows where she is?"

"She said she knows."

Monk nodded. "You came to the wrong place. I don't know your sister."

"But you know Breena. I need to find Breena."

Monk could hear the desperation in the billionaire's voice, even if he didn't appear desperate at all. But he was reeling, Monk could tell.

Monk studied him. "Why should I help you?" he asked.

"Because I need help," said Max. "And because you aren't unsavory enough to let my kid sister die when you could have provided some information."

"How would you know how the fuck I am?"

"Because Big Daddy Sinatra would not have allowed you to marry his daughter if you didn't have some redeeming qualities. Mick the Tick would not have either."

Monk stared at him. He had done his homework. And although he knew it was pure flattery to get what he wanted, that didn't mean he was wrong. "I deal with her," Monk admitted.

"In what capacity?" asked Max.

"She's a go-between when there are jobs to be done outside of my jurisdiction."

"You mean foreign jobs?"

Monk didn't respond which, Max, knew, meant yes. "Does it involve Albright?"

Monk frowned. "What's Albright?"

If he didn't know, Albright wasn't involved, which was good for Max's deal. "Who does she act as a go-between for?"

Monk paused. He had his own issues with the man. "Victor Slavitt," he said.

Max knew that name. "The arms

dealer?" Hood looked at Max. "Why would Breena be a go-between for an arms dealer?" Max asked.

But Monk was shaking his head. "You'll have to ask her that question."

"How do you know her?" Hood asked.

"And you are?"

"Mrs. Cassidy," said Max. "My wife."

"I know her, let's just keep it that way," Monk said, answering her question.

"Is she your girlfriend?" Hood asked.

"No," said Monk.

"Your ex-girlfriend?"

Monk hesitated. "Something like that," he said.

Max stared at him. He could tell Monk had been smitten by Breena once upon a time too, even though he was nicknamed The Monk for his lack of womanizing. But Max knew he needed to play on that *once upon a time feeling* Monk might still have for Breena. "She's missing," Max said. "There was blood. Which means she's in trouble too. I need to find her."

"Go to Victor Slavitt. He's nobody you should fear. He'll know where to find her."

"Is he here in Jersey?"

Monk shook his head. "No. He's in Chicago."

Although it meant another two hour flight,

Max was glad to hear that. Back on his own home turf. He stood up. "Text me his address," he said.

But old school Monk reached over on his desk, grabbed a slip of paper and a pen and wrote down the address, and then handed it to Max.

Max and Hood stood up. Max extended his hand. "Thanks," he said.

"Victor Slavitt is a bad man," said Monk, shaking the hand. "Don't thank me now because you won't thank me later."

"I thought you said we shouldn't fear him," said Hood.

"You shouldn't. But that doesn't mean he's a good guy."

Max and Hood both wondered what he meant by that doublespeak, but they had a mission, and this bad man was the only way they could get to where they needed to go. They took off.

But as soon as they made it out of the diner, Max felt his hairs lift on the back of his neck. Something wasn't right. He could feel it before he could see it. And then he saw it. A car driving slowly toward them. His heart dropped.

He moved in front of Hood. "Go back into the diner," he ordered her.

Hood heard that sound in Max's voice that made clear he meant business. Instead of asking why the way she was programmed to ask, she just did as she was told and hurried back into the diner.

But just as she left Max's side, Max saw the window on that car come down quickly and then he saw the beginnings of an assault rifle coming out. He knew, to protect Hood's retreat, he had to fire first to distract them from her. He pulled out his own gun and fired repeatedly as he dived for cover in front of his SUV. The rifle began firing back, but not at Max in front of that SUV, but at the entrance, and then the windows, of Monk's diner. The bullets were flying left and right, taking out every window and putting holes in every inch of that establishment. And Max's heart was in his shoe. Because he'd just ordered Hood back inside that diner. When that diner seemed to be the target of the hit!

Max couldn't move. He could barely breath. But he knew he had to wait it out. That assault rifle would get off twenty rounds to one round from his Glock and he knew it. But as soon as he heard what sounded like a clicking, which indicated to him that the rifle had fired its last bullet, he jumped up from behind that SUV and started firing on that car. The car began speeding away and Max was shooting as he ran after that car. The older men inside Monk's diner came out firing at that getaway car too. But the car was too fast. It got away.

But Max had Hood on his mind as he ran back into the diner. It had been shot up as badly inside as it looked on the outside, but Monk, to Max's relief, had his own body shielding Hood against the back wall. They didn't stand a chance to defend themselves, either, at the suddenness of that onslaught. And although two men were down because of cuts from flying glass, nobody was shot. Max ran to Hood as Monk ran to his downed men to make sure they were okay.

"Hood?"

Hood was nodding. "I'm okay. He grabbed me when he saw me run back inside." But it was Max Hood was worried about. She looked at him. "Are you okay?"

Max nodded. But Hood could still see the terror in his eyes.

Monk could see it too when he realized his men were going to be alright and he made it back over to Max and Hood. Max Cassidy was a tough guy, but he was out of his lane. This was Monk's lane. And they needed help.

"Maybe I need to be the go-between to get you to the airport," he said.

And Max and Hood weren't about to

object to that.

But Monk still couldn't reconcile the scene. "It's amazing you survived that barrage," he said.

But that was the part Max couldn't figure out either. "They weren't shooting at me," he said. "I was right there, but I wasn't the target at all."

"Are you implying they came for me?" asked Monk.

But Max had an even darker thought. "Or somebody else in this diner," he said.

And they both looked at Hood.

CHAPTER THIRTY

As soon as Max and Hood got back onto Max's plane, they retired to the bedroom for the two-hour flight back home. They were so emotionally spent they were just drained. They were lying there, side by side, facing each other.

"But why would they have targeted me?" asked Hood.

"I don't know. But that's what it felt like. I was right there for the taking, but they passed on me."

Hood shook her head. "But why?" she asked.

"I don't know. But we'll find out."

"And Breena. What if she's back in New York and we'll heading back to Chicago?" asked Hood.

"I have men surveilling her hotel and I have men waiting for her inside her suite should she show back up there. But so far there's been no sightings. We need to find out what this Victor Slavitt knows. We have to go where the names are. Monk gave me his name. We've got to follow up on that."

Hood hesitated, but decided to speak the truth. "She's very beautiful," she said.

Max wasn't going to disagree with that truth. "Yes," he said. "On the outside there's none more beautiful." Then he smiled a weary smile and touched the side of Hood's smooth face. "But you've got her beat."

"Me? How so?"

"You're beautiful inside and out."

Hood heard the compliment, but that wasn't what she was after. She continued to stare at him. "Do you love her?"

Max had to think about that question too. "A part of me might. I don't know," he said honestly.

"But why would she run like that?" Hood asked. "That's what I don't understand."

"Her handlers may have grown tired of her and decided to intervene. They obviously were in that suite with her."

"The guards said she was alone."

"Those guards didn't know where to look."

"But you don't think your sister was there, and that could have been her blood?"

"No," Max said. "That video I saw of her didn't take place in any hotel suite. And I doubt if they would risk moving her now."

"I still don't understand why they would suddenly grow tired of Breena when she was so close to hearing your decision."

"I mentioned the past. It has something to do with the day Jen was taken. And they panicked. That's the only reasonable explanation."

Hood nodded her head. She agreed with that assessment. She also agreed that Max was so strung out on pure emotion that she knew he needed some serious relaxation.

She moved down between his legs and began unbuckling and unzipping his pants. His penis, she could tell, was hardening as she was unzipping him. And by the time she pulled it out, it was as long and thick as it was rock hard.

But just as she was about to put it in her mouth, Max pulled her up on top of him, pulled down her jeans, and began fingering her. They kissed passionately as he did her. And as soon as she was dripping wet and groaning to the feelings, he entered her with a hard thrust in.

But she wasn't about to let him do all the work again. She sat up, on top of him, straddling him, and began to ride that rod that was deep inside of her, which caused Max to begin moaning and groaning too.

They could hear the swishing of the liquids as she rode his rod, and if relaxing was what she wanted for Max, she got it. He was coming down from that mountain of grief and anger and pain and fear. He was relaxing if only for those few moments.

And when his relaxing became intense with a different brand of emotions, the kind that had his dick throbbing and her vagina pulsating, he pulled her down into his arms and took over. And when Max took over, it was like going from the intensity of a small gunshot, to the intensity of a shotgun blast. Max pounded her.

They were moaning and groaning and the bedsprings were bouncing and groaning too as they made the kind of hard love that ensured a hard cum. And when it happened, when Hood first and then Max began to leave all out, they both lifted up in an altered state of release.

And although the actual cum lasted seconds, they still felt the reverberations from the intensity of that cum for several minutes more. Until their bodies came back down to earth, and collapsed under the weight of the strain and the drain and the remembrance of what was ahead of them.

But Max found the strength to hold onto Hood as they laid back down. "Thanks."

Hood leaned up and looked at him. "What are you thanking me for?"

"For being here," said Max, "just when I needed you most." He removed a strand of hair from her beautiful forehead. "Thank you."

"Where you go, I go?"

Max smiled. "Yes."

"Because I got your back, Max. Whatever danger, I got your back better than anybody else can have it. Whatever danger, we face it together."

Max even nodded on that. He knew Hood could handle herself. She had to when she was a kid. She had to when she was in Utah. But Max knew he had to give her conditions. "But you face that danger only with me," he said to her. "Not with Ricky. Not with Rita. You face it only when I'm there to protect you."

"And I'm there to protect you."

Max was inwardly amused at how little faith Hood had in his gangster abilities. "Yes," he said. "Only when we're together. But," he added.

Hood stared at him. "But what?"

"I'm Batman and you're Robin. And it will always be that way."

Hood laughed, but then her laughter was gone. Because it wasn't a laughing matter to her. It was a reaffirmation that they were in this thing together. No matter what.

And then she nodded her head with such a serious look on her face that it made Max feel as if they had just struck a deal. "I can live with that," she said to him. And then she collapsed, once again, into his arms.

CHAPTER THIRTY-ONE

Max's plane was just landing at the Chicago airfield as Jason Bogart, along with Dale Perry, was stepping out of the big, black Ford Expedition SUV.

"You think he'll let me take it from here after his New Jersey excursion," asked Dale, "and the shootout that happened at Monk Paletti's place?"

"You're his security chief," said Jason. "You tell me."

"You're his best friend," Dale shot back. "You tell me."

Jason looked at Dale. "Not a chance," he said, honestly answering his question.

Dale nodded his head. "Yeah, I figured as much too. He hates being surrounded by security."

"Get a clandestine detail on him though," ordered Jason. "After what happened in New Jersey, and until we figure out what these people want, I don't want you to take any chances with Max or Mrs. Cassidy."

"It's going to take a couple hours to pull a team together, since everybody thought he'd still be out of town."

"You and I will be his security until then," said Jason.

Dale looked at the operations chief suspiciously. Jason hailed from a rich, prep school kind of family just as Max hailed from. "You know your way around a gun, sir?" he asked him.

Jason looked at him. "Is snow white? Of course I know my way around a gun, are you kidding me?"

Dale laughed. "Just wanted to see your reaction," he said. "But you know Mr. C doesn't like security around him."

"That's why they must stay in the shadows or he'll pull'em. Make certain they stay out of sight."

Dale nodded as he pulled out his phone to make the call.

"And even if Max finds out about it," Jason said, "still keep it undercover. I don't care how much he objects."

That was easy for Jason to say, Dale thought. He was the man's best friend. But if Maxwell Cassidy objected under Dale's watch, there was no way he was going along with it anyway. No way. But he didn't tell Jason, who was ultimately his boss too, any of that.

When Jason saw Max and Hood deplane, he felt a surge of relief. They were back home and in one piece! But as soon as they got into the SUV, with Dale seated on the front seat beside Dobbs their driver, and Jason, Hood, and Max seated on the middle seat, his relief went out the window when Max told Dobbs where to take him.

"A laundromat?" asked Jason.

"Yes."

"But why? Clothes dirty?"

"There's a guy there I need to check out."

"What guy?"

Max exhaled, because he knew Jason would know that name too. "Victor Slavitt," he said.

Jason turned to Max as if he'd lost his mind. "You and Hood are going to see an international arms dealer, Max? Are you bonkers?"

Dale steeled himself for the onslaught. Max never let anybody talk to him that way.

But Max wasn't in the combative mood. He had to find his sister. "According to Monk Paletti, he should know where to locate Breena. And Breena can lead me to Jenny. I'm not leaving it to anybody else to handle this job but me. And my wife," he added, to Hood's delight.

"But Max! Why are you dragging Hood along with you?"

"He's not dragging me anywhere," said

Hood. "So you can pump your brakes on that right now, Jason. I want to go with him. I can handle a gun, and myself, as good as anybody else."

Max smiled. "That's why," he said to Jason. Because Max knew she wasn't exaggerating. He had total faith in her ability to have his back. But he mostly wanted her with him because he instinctively knew she'd be safer with him than with any other guard. And because he felt that way, that settled it. They went straight to the address Monk had given them.

But Hood was confused when they drove up to such a dilapidated-looking laundromat in old Chinatown. She looked at Hood. "We found The Monk at a diner. Now an international arms dealer is hiding out at this laundromat?"

"Who's hiding?" asked Max. "He's just a man operating a laundromat. What's he hiding for?"

Jason laughed. Hood shook her head. She never understood how gangsters got away with such obvious front businesses and never would.

They got out, with Jason and Dale supplying high price security for the couple, as the foursome entered the laundromat.

Inside, it was easy to spot their target.

Everybody else inside appeared to be Chinese women sorting through huge piles of clothing. They walked up to the fat white man behind the counter.

"Can I help you?"

"You can if you're Victor Slavitt," said Max.

The man said nothing.

"Are you Slavitt?"

"Who's asking?"

"Maxwell Cassidy."

"I don't know no Maxwell Cassidy."

"The Monk sent us," said Hood. "Know him?"

The man looked at Hood as if she was the only one of those stuff shirts that spoke his language. "New customers, are you?"

"You can say that, yes," said Hood.

The man looked at Hood again, and then at Max, Jason, and Dale. "Let's talk in my office," he said and escorted them down the hall where a table was located. He sat down. Max and Hood sat down too. Jason and Dale remained standing, looking around.

And Max didn't beat around the bush. "You're Victor Slavitt?"

"That's right."

"Where's Breena?"

But Victor Slavitt frowned. "I don't know

any Breena."

To Dale and Jason's shock, Hood jumped up, with her Glock drawn, and put it to Victor's head. "Does this refresh your memory?" she asked him.

Victor knew that black chick had some gangster in her. Couldn't say the same about the guys. But he could tell that girl had it in her. And he nodded. "I think I do know a little something about a Breena or somebody like that."

"Where is she?" Max asked him.

"Now that I don't know."

Max jumped up and placed his own Glock to the other side of Victor's head. "Where is she?" he said forcefully.

But Victor's entire countenance changed. And he suddenly held up his hands as if they were the cops.

"What are you doing that for?" asked Max. "Just tell me where she is."

Still Victor said nothing.

Max frowned. "What the fuck is wrong with you? You think we're playing with your ass?"

Then Victor's already pop eyeballs slanted as if he was trying to get their attention further down the hallway. All of them caught onto it quickly. Max pointed his weapon at Hood and at Jason, and then he pointed his weapon at Victor as he looked at Dale. They all understood: Hood and Jason were to go down that hall with Max, because he trusted both of them with his life, and Dale was to stay with Victor Slavitt.

Dale quickly placed his gun against Victor's head, and began talking as if they were still trying to get him to say where Breena was. Victor was cooperating, saying repeatedly that he didn't know where she was, as Max, Hood, and Jason, with their guns drawn, made their way down that long, narrow hall.

There was one door at the end of the hall, but another door was closer. Max turned toward Victor as they arrived at that door and pointed his weapon at it. When Victor nodded, Jason went on the left side, Max stayed on the right side, and Max pulled Hood behind him. It wasn't her preferred position but she knew she had to do whatever Max told her to do or he'd never allow her on any other search runs with him ever again. She stayed behind him.

And then Max made sure Jason was ready, took a deep breath, and then he violently kicked the door open with his shoe.

The door flung open and he and Jason hurried across the threshold aiming their weapons with both hands, and ready to fire.

But what they found stunned Max. Breena was in that room, alright, but she had been so badly beaten that it appeared she'd been tortured. That same white gown she had taken off at her hotel suite, was back on her body but it was in tatters. She was tied down in a chair, and every inch of her body was bruised. Her head was slanted sideways. Her eyes were rolling backwards, and she seemed to be drifting in and out of consciousness.

But Max knew he had to keep his wits about him. Breena was as slick as oil and he knew it.

When Hood looked around Max and saw Breena, she was as shocked as he was. They could lose her and in so doing lose any chance of finding Max's sister, so she hurried past Max to see what she could do for Breena.

While Hood was doing that, Max and Jason searched the small room but found nobody else. They found drills and whips and canes and plenty of other torture equipment that they could tell was used on Breena, but they didn't find anybody else.

"She needs a doctor, Max," Hood said as she was knelt down to Breena. "She's not gonna make it if we don't get her some help."

But before Max could respond, he heard a sound out in the hall.

He and Jason hurried out in the hall and looked toward Victor first, which was where they thought they heard the noise. But Dale still had control of Victor.

Max and Jason then looked in the opposite direction, at that door further down the hall, and that was when they saw Jennifer, standing just outside of that door, staring at them.

Max's heart dropped. "Jen?" he asked. He was in pure shock. Jason was too.

But when Jen was quickly snatched into that room at the end of the hall, both men snapped out of it, Max ordered Hood to stay put, and they ran toward that room.

But this time Max didn't waste a second with any set up for entry. He flung that door open, which led to a room filled with dry-cleaned clothes on racks. Max and Jason ran through that room, knocking those racks aside, until they ran to another door.

But just as Max flung that door open, revealing that the door led outside to the back of the laundromat, a gunshot was fired that caught the door's hinge and forced Max to pull Jason back as he pulled back behind the door too. And then, after that initial shot, there was a barrage of bullets that they both knew was coming from an assault rifle that no way they could match.

They both dropped down and Max had to kick the door back shut while they scurried to get away from the onslaught.

There was a closet near the door and they both hurried inside, as the barrage continued unabated for what seemed like years to Max, but was only a few seconds longer.

But as soon as the gunfire stopped, they hurried to the door, opened it, and saw the very tail end of a car. But then they saw Jen in the backseat turning around and looking at them, as the car sped away.

Max and Jason were both mortified that they could lose her again as they ran after that car. Max, unable to accept such a harsh reality, outran Jason easily. But by the time they got out of the backyard of that laundromat and onto the side street, the car had completely disappeared. There was no sight of it at all.

"Go get Dobbs!" Max yelled at Jason.

"Max, they're gone," Jason said back.

"Go get Dobbs!"

Jason turned Max around angrily. "They're gone, Max! Dobbs can't do shit. They're gone!"

Max knew it too. And he knew his desperation was showing. But he also knew who could give him answers.

As Jason got on the phone, asking Dale

if the clandestine crew he ordered had arrived, Max ran back into the building, back through that dry-cleaning room, and back down the hall to the room where Breena was located.

As soon as he entered that room, Hood, who was standing at the door guarding it, was asking if he was okay. But Max was on a mission. He ran over to Breena like a mad man and started shaking her violently. "Who has Jen?" he asked her. "Tell me who has Jen!"

"Max, you'll kill her," Hood said, trying to pull him away from her.

"Tell me who has my sister!" he yelled.

"Max!" Hood yelled at him, grabbing him by his massive bicep. "If she dies we won't know anything. Max, stop!"

And only then did he stop. Because Hood was right. Breena was in no position to tell them anything.

Jason hurried into the room. "We got a crew searching for a black car, since that's all I saw of it, but at least they're searching."

But Max wasn't waiting around for any crew to assemble. He ran out of the room. Hood, worried sick about Max, ran behind him. They both ran up front, to Victor.

And as soon as they got there, Hood knew what Max was going to do. And she did it too. They both, once again, placed their Glocks against each side of Victor's head, muscling Dale out of the way.

"Who has my sister?" Max said with clenched teeth.

But Victor said nothing. Although Jen and whomever had her were gone, Victor seemed to look even more terrified.

"Tell me!" Max screamed and placed his gun so hard against the side of Victor's head that it began to draw blood.

"Okay," Victor said. "I'll tell you everything, but don't shoot me because you're scared."

Max and Dale stopped aiming their guns at Victor. But Hood kept her gun trained on him.

Victor saw it too. "I don't wanna get shot," he said to Hood.

"Just talk!" Hood yelled. "Stop worrying about what I'm doing and tell us who has Jennifer!"

Max looked at Hood and nodded. He was proud of her. He was glad he had her by his side or he might have lost it in that room with Breena.

"Okay," Victor said. "Let's just calm down folks."

But as soon as he opened his mouth to tell them, and they all waited anxiously to hear what he had to say, he grabbed a small gun that was strapped beneath the table where he sat, put it in his mouth, and fired before even Hood could react.

Max pushed Hood back and backed up too as Victor's head rolled side to side and then just leaned backward. Blood was gushing out of his mouth.

Max grabbed Hood and buried her head in his chest. He hated that she was there to witness that. But he looked at Dale. Who would be so afraid that they'd kill themselves rather than tell what they knew?

But when they began to hear sirens, Max knew he only had one choice. If the cops got involved, everything would go in slow motion.

With Hood at his side, he ran back into the room where Breena was still fighting for her life. And this time even Hood knew he had to get an answer. "Who has my sister?" he said to her in a voice that screamed desperation. "You're the only one can help me, Bree. Who has Jen?!"

Although she was still in dire straits, Breena's eyes stopped rolling backwards when she heard Max's desperate plea. And she tried her best to talk, but it was only a whisper. Max hurried closer to her, to hear that whisper. "Dee," she barely said. "Elm," she barely added. "Dee Elm," she whispered again as they could hear the police running into the building.

But Max was lost. "Who's Dee Elm?" he asked her frantically. "Who is she?"

"Goes," she said. "Part," she added breathlessly.

And then the police ran into the room yelling for everybody in that room to put their hands up.

Max and Hood dropped their weapons and did as they were told.

But Max was so perplexed he didn't know what to do. Who was Dee Elm? And what did she mean by goes part? The cops were frisking them, and calling for an ambulance for Breena, but all Max heard were those words Breena had whispered to him. And all he saw was Jen's face in that hall and then turning around in that car. He saw her. She wasn't fifteen feet away from him looking as stunned to see him as he was to see her. And he failed her. *Again.*

CHAPTER THIRTY-TWO

Max and Hood were in the living room of their home, with Rita, Ricky, and Rita's son Timmy summoned over to keep them under protection should this craziness extend to them, but also Max wanted them there to comfort Hood. She had seen too much. And he was blaming himself for that lapse in judgment too.

Hood and her siblings were on the sofa, while Timmy sat on the floor at his mother's feet. Hood had already told what all had happened, and they were in a collective state of shock. Rita and Ricky both were angry at Max for exposing their baby sister to such dangerous situations and around such dangerous people, but they knew they had to be careful with the man who was also their boss.

But Rita didn't care. "You wanted to take her head off for beating up a guy who beat me up, but you have no problem taking her around mob bosses and arms dealers? Are you serious, Max?"

"I'm saying," Ricky said, agreeing with his sister. Enough was enough. "I know we're nothing but your workers, and if we didn't work for you we would barely have a pot to piss in or a window to throw that shit out, but Hood is our sister. And nobody's mistreating our sister. Hood could have been killed," Ricky said forcefully.

"Killed," agreed Timmy.

"Max was with me," said Hood. "He had my back and I had his."

"We know you think you can handle any kind of situation," said Rita. "You never back down from a fight. But Max shouldn't have put you in that position. He was wrong for that. For real though."

Max stopped pacing, placed his hands in his pockets, and nodded his head. "You're right," he said to the Rileys. "She saw too much today. I should have known not to let her go, but I wanted her with me. I knew she would be okay if she was with me. But . . . I was scared."

They all stared at Max. They'd never seen him admit any fault whatsoever.

"Knowing that my sister is still out there alive scared the shit out of me," Max continued. "I was scared I'd blow it again, since it was my careless ass that allowed her to be taken in the first place, and I needed Hood by my side. She knows how to focus me on the big picture. She knows how to make me feel as if I can handle anything. She knows how to protect me."

When Max said those words, the Rileys

were stunned. Max Cassidy felt Hood could protect *him*?

But Hood wasn't surprised by Max's confidence in her abilities. She got up and went to him, and placed her hands on the sides of Max's face. His face was just overtaken with anguish. And Hood's heart dropped. She hugged him.

"I lost her again, Hood," Max started saying in a voice dripping with pain. "I lost her again!"

But when Hood heard that voice, she pulled him back and looked into his eyes. "You haven't lost her yet," she said. "Because you've got to stop living in the past and stop worrying about what you did or didn't do. You've got to think, Max. Who's Dee Elm? What does *goes part* mean? We'll find her, but you've got to stop feeling sorry for yourself and figure this out!"

They all knew Hood could be hard as steel. But in this instance, they all also knew that she was right.

"Sit down and think," said Hood.

Max sat down in a chair, and Hood knelt down at the chair beside him. "Do you know anybody called Dee Elm?" asked Hood. "Or anybody with the initial D?"

But Max was searching the rolodex of his brain, as he'd already been doing. "No. I don't know anybody with that name."

"What about goes part? Does that mean anything to you?"

But Max was shaking his head again. "No. Nothing."

"Maybe they meant Gospart," said Timmy. "Maybe it's somebody's last name. Know anybody with that last name, Uncle Max?"

"No," Max said.

"But it has to mean something, Max," said Hood, "or Breena wouldn't have said those words to you if she knew you didn't know anything about them."

Max knew she was right, but none of it rang a bell.

"Think back to when your sister was kidnapped," said Rita. "Maybe it was something back then."

"Yeah, Max," said Hood. "You said those people probably moved Breena out of that hotel suite because you mentioned the day Jen was kidnaped to her. Look back."

"I am looking back." Max's voice was agitated now. "That's all I've been doing is looking back and I'm telling you I've never heard of any Dee Elm or goes par or - - -." Max stopped mid-sentence, as if he'd just realized something major.

Hood and her family all realized it too.

"What is it?" Hood asked him. "What is it, Max?"

"Not goes," Max said. "She wasn't saying goes. She was trying to say Joe's," he said instead.

"Joe's?"

"And not part. She was trying to say partner, but she barely had the breath to say it."

"Joe's partner?" asked Timmy.

"Joe's partner."

But Ricky still was puzzled. "But who's Joe?"

Max looked at him as if he'd asked the relevant question. "My father," said Max. "His name was Joseph. Joe."

"And he had a partner named Dee Elm?"

"He had a partner named Dave Minor. She wasn't saying Dee Elm. She was trying to say DM."

"People called your father's partner DM?" asked Hood.

"I don't know what nicknames he had. I didn't hang around my old man's business like that. And when he died and I inherited Cassidy-Minor, I bought Dave Minor out. I didn't want to partner with him any longer. He agreed, but I had to agree to keep the company's name. To keep his name as part of the company."

"Why didn't you want to partner with him?" Rita asked.

Max thought about it. Then he remembered why not. "He always seemed shady to me."

"Wow," said Ricky.

"So you think Breena was saying," Hood asked Max, "that your father's business partner has your sister?"

"That's the only thing I can figure it out to be," said Max.

"But why would your father's business partner kidnap your sister, Uncle Max?" asked Timmy.

Max didn't know. "Maybe I'm way off base," he said, running his hands through his hair. "Maybe I don't know what the fuck I'm talking about."

"Were your father and his partner enemies?" asked Hood.

"No. They were best friends. They did everything together. My father wouldn't have ever thought Dave would do something like that."

"Those are the ones who do it," said Rita.

"I'm saying," agreed Ricky.

"And you said yourself," Ricky added, "that the man seemed shady to you."

"And if not him," asked Hood, "then who?"

But Max couldn't answer that question.

He got on his feet again, pacing again, doing all he could to see if there was any other explanation other than the one he thought of.

Until Dale, who was outside supervising the gate and grounds security teams, came hurrying inside the house.

"Just got a call from Jason at the hospital, sir," he said as soon as he saw Max's face.

Everybody looked at him. Hood stood up.

"What did he say?" asked Max.

"Breena's awake and able to talk. She wants to see you."

Max looked at Hood. Now, he prayed, they'd get answers! He grabbed Hood by the hand and ran for the exit. Rita and Ricky and Timmy didn't hesitate. It was a family thing now. They made a run for it too.

CHAPTER THIRTY-THREE

It was the first time the Rileys were seeing this Breena person, and all three of them were amazed when they saw her. Even with the scars of a *hit-by-a-train* kind of beating, her beauty still shined through. She was still a sight to behold. Ricky and Rita looked at each other. How could Hood compete against somebody that looked like that?

Rita was also surprised that she was a black lady. Somehow she figured Max to be one of those *rich white girls* kind of guy who just so happened to fall in love with a poor black girl. She just assumed it was the magic of Hood, the kid sister she adored, rather than some preference of Max's. Which made Rita look at Max in a completely different light. There were so many layers to the man, she felt, that she was only just beginning to scratch the surface of who Max truly was.

But what Max and Hood realized when they walked into that hospital room had nothing to do with Breena's beauty nor her race. They realized that Breena was fully awake now and appeared fully alert, and her hospital bed was slanted up, which allowed her to sit up in bed. They were both relieved, because they needed answers to find Jen, and they hurried to her bedside.

Jason, along with Tish Holmes, his assistant, were already in the room, as Max had asked Jason to be there should Breena wake up. To give Max some space to question Breena, they went over to greet the Rileys.

But Max and Hood had no time to do anything but seek answers. They had to find Jen!

"Is it Dave Minor?" Max asked as soon as they made it to Breena's bedside. Hearing that name, a name Jason knew since childhood, shocked him. He looked at Breena too.

When Hood saw how Breena's entire face changed, she knew Max had hit that nail on the head.

"I need everyone to leave," Breena said in a voice surprisingly strong, considering how weak it was just a few hours ago.

And Jason didn't hesitate. "Alright, you heard the lady. Everybody out," he said as Rita and Ricky, along with Timmy and Tish and Jason himself began to make their way out.

Hood was about to leave, too. She

understood the importance of getting whatever information Breena could give. But Max pulled her back. "She stays with me," he said.

Breena shook her head. "This doesn't concern her," she said.

"If it concerns me, it concerns her. She stays with me," Max said again. And by the way he said it, even Breena knew there was no changing his mind.

"We'll be in the waiting room," said Jason and left with the others, closing the door behind him.

"Is it Dave Minor?" Max asked again anxiously.

"Yes," Breena said. "It was DM."

Her confirmation seemed to only confuse Max more. "But how?" he asked, unable to even comprehend such a thing. Dave Minor was his father's best friend!

"DM and his wife were having dinner with your parents that night, so he ordered me to phone you and ask if you wanted to hook up. You told me to come right over, and so I did. He also ordered me to get you upstairs and do what I do, and for me to leave the front door unlocked. When you went to get ice cream for Jen, I unlocked the door."

Max knew he had locked that door! But after what happened to Jen, he spent a lifetime second-guessing himself.

"But why would Dave Minor be ordering you to do anything?" asked Max. "How would you even know him?"

Then Max realized how. "He was one of your sugar daddies?" he asked her.

But Breena didn't answer that question. And it didn't matter to Max. "Where does he have Jen?" he asked Breena.

But she shook her head. "I don't know. I never knew where he kept her."

"But you knew, all these years, he had her?"

Breena seemed to hate admitting it. "Yes."

"Why wouldn't you tell me, Bree? You saw how it destroyed every ounce of me. I thought you . . ."

"I did love you," said Breena proudly. "I still love you," she admitted.

Hood's heart did sank. She knew she couldn't compete against somebody like Breena Novak. But it wasn't about her nor Breena. She had to keep her eye on the ball. "But why would his business partner and best friend kidnap a little girl?" Hood asked.

Breena looked at Hood for seemingly the first time since their arrival. She looked like her name to Breena, with those big-ass, suspicious eyes. But what surprised her was that Hood seemed savvy, in a street sort of way.

"Why, Bree?" Max asked too. "Why would Dave snatch Jen?"

"Money," Breena said. "He was in freefall with all the gambling and overextensions he had done in his life. He was on the verge of personal bankruptcy. He needed the cash."

"And instead of asking my father, he what? Kidnaps his best friend's daughter?"

"He did ask your father to let him get money out of their business reserves, but your father, who was far and away the majority owner, would never sign off on it. And yes, he used Jen to get what he needed."

"But how did he do it?"

"He and his wife went out to dinner with your parents and ordered me to make sure I unlocked the door and distract you upstairs while Toby was downstairs snatching the girl."

Max frowned. "Who's Toby?"

"Toby Fitch. Some evil bastard Dave always used to do his dirty work. He still uses him." Breena used Toby as well, but she didn't mention that fact.

"It was supposed to be just for a few hours. They demanded the four million dollars ransom, your father would pay it, and that would be that. But when your father didn't pay the ransom," Breena added, "everything changed."

Hood was shocked. "Your father wouldn't pay the ransom? I thought you said he paid it?"

Max was confused too. "He did pay it. What are you talking about, Bree? He paid every dime they asked for, but they took the money and never produced my sister."

"That was a lie," said Breena. "DM had your old man under surveillance the entire time. I even saw the video myself. He went to the bank and withdrew the money, alright, and when they called and told him where to drop it off after he secured it, he told them okay, but he never showed up at the drop-off site. He just drove around town, went into a parking garage and placed the money in the boot of his car, and went back home. He told that lie about how they took the money but never gave him Jennifer. He kept that money."

Max could hardly believe what he was hearing. "But why would he endanger his own daughter like that?"

But Hood already had a good idea why. "Because she wasn't his daughter?" she asked Breena.

Max looked at Hood as if she'd lost her mind. What the fuck was she talking about?

But Breena nodded her head. "That's right," she said.

Max looked at Breena. "She is his daughter!" he proclaimed.

"DM and your mother had a long-term affair. It lasted years. And your father knew about it. When they took the DNA test to determine paternity, and it was confirmed that DM was the father, your old man knew about that too. But for appearances sake, they listed your father on the birth certificate and told the world she was his child too. But she wasn't. He probably was glad to be rid of what DM said he viewed as his wife's shame. But because he didn't pay, and because he was willing to endanger Jen's life, DM was furious with your father."

"He confronted him?" Hood asked.

Breena shook her head. "No." She looked at Max. "He killed him."

Hood looked at Max in horror too. Even she hadn't expected to hear that! But Max was floored. "He *what*?"

"He killed him. Or at least had him killed. He paid Toby Fitch to tamper with his brakes and then, when he was driving up in those mountains the way he does most weekends, he had Toby force him off the road and watch his car go over the cliff and burst into flames. It was ruled an accident, but it was no accident. DM bought and paid for that death."

Max was so overcome with shock he didn't know where to begin to comprehend it.

But Hood was staring at Breena. What kind of friend was she? "You knew this all these years," she said to her, "but you never told Max? And he said you took off instead of helping them find his sister after that ransom was paid, or wasn't paid. How could you do that to him?"

"Because it was being done to me!" Breena said angrily, and Max looked at her. "You said that kidnapping destroyed you," she said to Max, "but DM was destroying me. And torturing me. And made me watch him kill this girl my age because she disrespected him, and he had all these mafia friends who did all these despicable things in front of me. And they all made it clear to me that if I ever disobeyed DM, I'd be next. And my family back in Mississippi. My parents, Max, would be next. So they used me. I was their go-between for arms sells and drug drops or whatever else needed done."

"Was Monk Paletti one of those mob guys?"

Breena shook her head. "He was the only one who wasn't. That's why I was always happy to be the go-between when he needed foreign jobs handled. He was the only one who didn't abuse me."

Then she shook her head. "But

everybody else were just evil. I was their mule when they needed to get certain drugs into the US. I did it all for them. And DM never stopped reminding me of what I faced if I strayed for a second. He was an awful man. And I was terrified of him."

"But Max would have helped you," said Hood.

"Max?" She was offended. "Max didn't have shit either back then! He had what his old man doled out to him and nothing more. And when his old man died and he dropped out of college to take care of the family business, I wasn't allowed to be around him. Except when DM needed information. And I was always wired with a microphone those few times, usually in my wig or I used my phone to record our conversations and whatever else we were doing. Then he married Camille and wouldn't cheat on her. But when Camille and Amber died, and after Max recovered from his injuries, DM wouldn't let me within a thousand feet of Max."

She looked at Max. "He knew I was in love with you, and that's why I never saw you again. He moved to Prague and took me with him. And he got me employed at Albright because the CEO owed one of his mobster friends. I never looked back. Because he wouldn't let me. He had connections everywhere. They would have killed me and my family just as sure as I'm laying here if I disobeyed him. I was a prisoner with invisible chains. But I was locked up too."

"But why was he in Chicago?" asked Max. "Why did he have Jen in Chicago?"

"He wasn't in Chicago."

Max and Hood both were confused. "Then who tortured you?" asked Hood.

"And who took you from that hotel suite in New York?" asked Max.

"DJ," said Breena.

Max knew who DJ was. "Dave, Junior?" he asked Breena.

Breena nodded. "He'd been at his father's side the entire time. He was just as psychotic and evil as DM. Maybe more so. When DM died last month in Prague, DJ wouldn't allow the authorities to even announce his father's death."

Max was surprised. "Dave Minor's dead?"

"He died last month. That's why you were suddenly back in the picture. Dave didn't give a shit about you. It was DJ who blamed your family for every ill fortune his family ever faced. And when DM died, he decided to get his revenge. He wanted to destroy your marriage so that you would want me again. And then he planned for me to take you for every dime you were worth and give it all to him. He had me wired the entire time. I couldn't do anything without DJ knowing about it. He snatched me from that hotel suite when he thought I had failed to convince you of our plan. He took me to Chicago, to Victor Slavitt's laundromat, to kill me."

"Why did Slavitt kill himself?" Hood asked.

"Because they had his family, no doubt," answered Max.

Breena nodded. "If he snitched, DJ said he'd kill his little kids. He knew DJ had all those mob connections like DM had. Victor felt he had no way out either."

Max could hardly hear anymore. His entire world view had been rocked. But Jen was and had to be his first concern. "Where's Dave keeping Jen?" he asked Breena. "You have to know something!"

"But I told you I don't know. I don't know!"

"Where did he keep you?" asked Hood. "When you were here in Chicago?"

"Before we went to Prague, he kept me in New York. He had a place there."

This interested Max. "What kind of place?"

"An apartment. A very luxurious apartment. That's where we lived. That's why I never took you to my place. But after your plane crash, he heard me planning to meet up with you at that restaurant, and he beat the crap out of me. I was unconscious for days. Then he took me to Prague and I never came back. Until after his death and DJ wanted revenge."

"But DJ has Jen in Chicago. She was in that laundromat."

Breena nodded. "So?"

"So where were they staying in Chicago?"

"I don't know! I told you I don't know! I never knew."

Hood believed her. She could feel her anguish. But her anguish was nothing compared to Max's.

He began walking around that room, his hand rubbing the back of his neck, his face unable to figure out anything.

And it remained that way for several minutes. Until the door of that hospital room was opened, and a face Max would never forget walked in and stopped in his tracks too.

Max frowned. "DJ?" he said.

Dave Minor, Junior, also known as DJ, didn't expect to see Max in that room. His plan was to get Breena out of there before she could talk. But it looked as if she was already conscious and singing like a canary. And he knew he was facing the one man that could end it all for him. And he took off.

If what Breena said was true, Max knew DJ was all he had to get to Jen. He was the only link. And he took off after DJ with a determination that was not going to fail this time. He ran for his life. And Hood, who understood the stakes too, took off running after him.

Max saw DJ turn a corner at the end of the hospital hall and ran after him. Hood was a fast runner, but Max had the motivation. Which made him, in that moment, much quicker. He wasn't about to let DJ out of his sight not for a second. And he ran after DJ through corridor after corridor until DJ opened the door of a stairwell and ran into it.

Max pulled out his gun as he opened that corridor door. And as soon as he opened it, he was met with gunfire from DJ. He ducked back but didn't stop the pursuit the way he did at the laundromat. He went into that stairwell shooting back, which forced DJ to continue to run.

DJ and Max, with Hood not that far behind, ran down five flights of stairs in record time. And when DJ ran across the lobby and out of the revolving doors just as an announcement was being made about shots being heard in the stairwell, Max and Hood were out of the door ahead of the scared hospital workers and visitors who began to run out of the hospital too.

But DJ kept on running across the parking lot to a Mustang that sped up to pick him up. Toby Fitch was driving that Mustang.

Max knew he couldn't let DJ get into that car. "Stay back, Hood!" Max yelled as he lunged for that car just as DJ was getting inside. He held onto the door and had grabbed DJ's shirt. He was trying to drag DJ out of the moving vehicle, but DJ was fighting him off and attempting to pull out his gun.

When Toby pulled out his own revolver and shot at Max, causing Max to duck, Max still held onto that door and DJ's shirt. But Hood knew it was a losing battle and she pulled out her own gun to try and take out the tires.

But before she could get a shot off, Toby started swerving recklessly in that parking lot, hitting cars and almost pinning Max against the Mustang and another car, and then Toby fired another shot at Max. Although Max still held on: he was not about to let DJ go, the swerving threw him from the vehicle and down onto the pavement. Hood ran to him.

But Max jumped back up and tried to grab for the car again, but Toby had sped away.

DJ slammed the door shut that Max had

been holding onto. And as Toby turned onto the busy street to get away from there, DJ started pumping his fist out of the car's window as if he was defiantly showing that he got the better of Max Cassidy again. Even Toby was gleeful that they were getting away and taking their secret with them. A secret that had Max and Hood still running after the speeding car.

But Toby had only just turned onto the busy highway when he realized his gleefulness and inattention had caused him to turn into oncoming traffic. One car was able to swerve and avoid him. And two more cars avoided him too. But the flatbed truck in front of him didn't know he was coming while looking back at the traffic he avoided rather than the traffic ahead of him. Toby slammed into that flatbed with such force, that it not only killed him instantly, but it decapitated DJ. The flatbed of that truck had split that Mustang from top to bottom.

When the wreck occurred, and Max saw the decapitation and the massive amount of blood that splashed against the back of the car's window, he immediately turned Hood's face away from the carnage. There was no way she was seeing that!

But Max was devastated. He thought he was going to die right along with DJ. Because DJ's death meant the death of Jen. Nobody seemed to know but the man who was no longer on this earth where Jen was located. Max almost collapsed.

But he didn't. Because he had to hold up for Hood.

"Is he dead?" Hood was asking anxiously as Max refused to let her look. "Did he die?"

"Yes," Max said. "He's dead."

He could feel Hood's body try to collapse too, but he held her up. "How could this happen?" she was crying. "He's the only one that could lead us to where she is. What are we gonna do, Max? Where are we gonna find the will to keep searching for her when nobody knows where she is?"

The will, Max thought. He had to find the will to keep searching. He couldn't stop now! Jen was within his grasp. How could he stop now?

But as he looked at that wreckage and at the medical personnel running from the hospital to the scene, he started praying. "Lord, help me find my sister," he cried, his anguish unbearable. "Lord please help me. Don't let her disappear again. Please help me, Lord. Please!"

And as soon as he said that last word, he remembered what Hood had just said to him. And he grabbed her by the hand, ran to his

Porsche, and they jumped in.

It wasn't until he was tearing out of that parking lot, and onto the main highway, did Hood ask him what was happening.

"The will," he said.

"The will to keep searching?" She didn't know what he was getting at.

"My mother's will," said Max as he sped down the highway.

"What about your mother's will?"

"We moved out after Dad died. Mom couldn't bear to be in that house without Jen, and she closed it up and we moved away. And when she died, she left everything to me, but she left one thing to Dave."

"The house you grew up in?"

"Yes. But she didn't call it our family home in her will. She called it the scene of the crime."

Hood was shocked. "As if she knew Dave Minor was involved?"

Max was nodding his head. "I thought at the time it just meant it was the scene of Jen's kidnapping and she gave it to Dave because she knew I wouldn't want it. I had other siblings, but they were all my father's bastard children and she wasn't leaving a dime to them. So she left that house to Dave."

"It's here in Chicago?"

"My father's business was in California, but he and my mother were born and raised in Chicago so we lived between our house in Chicago and our house in California. But Mom left the house here in Chicago to Dave."

And as soon as Hood realized what Max was saying, and as soon as Max realized what that could mean, he picked up even more speed. He was praying, and Hood was praying that the house in that will was the answer they'd been looking for.

But her heart went out to Max. That guilt was riding him hard. So hard that she knew, if it wasn't resolved in a happy reunion with his kid sister, he was not going to be able to survive.

CHAPTER THIRTY-FOUR

They had to scale a brick wall that now surrounded the home to get on the other side, and security cameras were everywhere. But Max was betting that the only eyes viewing those cameras would be DJ's, and he wasn't viewing anything right now.

"This was your childhood home?" Hood asked as Max helped her down from the wall of the now dilapidated looking big house.

"It used to be beautiful," he said.

"But it got in the wrong hands,"

Max nodded. "Or the right hands. If Jen's inside. Because if she's anywhere else, I'm doomed."

Hood squeezed Max's arm. She understood.

But as they began hurrying toward the front door, their hopes seemed more like wishful thinking. That home barely looked inhabitable. There was a massive brick wall surrounding it, which kept it from being an eyesore to the rest of the neighborhood, but it was a hot mess in every way.

But this was all they had left. And as Max's stride increased, so did Hood's. She was slightly behind him, looking around, hoping and praying they weren't running to a boobytrap.

When they got to the front door, they saw a heavy burglar barred door, a door so heavy that nobody was getting inside of that. Max began to bang on that door.

Then he began looking around at the massive front windows. But they were all boarded up. He banged on those boards. But they were as thick as the front burglar bar door.

Then he ran through the high weeds of the lawn to the side of the house, with Hood running right behind him. All of those windows were boarded up too. Except for a small crack, as if whomever was inside had carved out a hole to look out of. And when Max looked inside, he at first saw nothing but the kitchen area he remembered so well. But when he looked to his right, his heart dropped.

"Jen!" he cried and began banging on the window. "Jen! She's in there, Hood," he said happily. "She's in there!"

Hood moved up to that crack to see for herself. And just as he said, she did see a blonde young lady sitting in a chair. But she also saw that the young lady was strapped to that chair, but it wasn't with tape.

"She's wired, Max," she said.

Max frowned. "Wired?"

"She's wired," Hood said as she stepped aside.

And when Max looked again and realized he didn't even see those wires the first time, that in his excitement he only saw Jen, his heart dropped again.

"What are we gonna do?" Hood asked him.

But Max knew he had to do something. "Call 911," he said to Hood.

"But there's a timer on it," Hood said, even as she was calling 911.

Max looked at that timer too. He could barely make it out, but it appeared to be two minutes and twenty-one seconds. Which meant, he knew, that there was precious little time!

"It can't be," he said, panic attempting to assert itself again. "Lord, let it not be so. Let it not be so!"

"What's the address, Max?" Hood asked. "The 911 operator needs the address."

As Max was giving Hood the address, it was then that he realized that this was his childhood home. And there were always ways of sneaking into that house that only he, as the person who grew up sneaking back in, knew about.

He tore off running toward the back yard. Hood was talking with the operator, but running behind Max.

And when they got to the backdoor, and saw that it had that thick burglar bar on it too, Max didn't hesitate. He began running down the steps that led to the basement. The only problem? There was no basement door. Just a brick wall.

"There's no entrance," Hood said as she ran down behind him. "What are we gonna do, Max?"

"Stand back," Max said.

Hood didn't understand why, but she moved back like she was told. And Max leaned back as far as he could, took his expensive shoe, and pressed against the brick wall. And within seconds, and to Hood's shock, it pushed open. Rich people, Hood thought, and all of these hidden doors!

Max, with Hood behind him, began running into the house.

The basement smelled of mold and wet clothing as Max and Hood ran across the floor and then up the stairs. All Max could think about was getting Jen out of there.

And as soon as they made it to the living room area, where Jen was tied down to a chair in the middle of the room, Jennifer Cassidy looked at Maxwell Cassidy as if she was just realizing that the first time she saw him at that laundromat wasn't a ghost like DJ told her it was.

"Maxwell?" she said to him in a voice not that unsimilar to her tiny, childhood voice. "Is that really you?"

Maxwell wanted to die where he stood. "It's me, Jen," he said, his voice trembling.

"There's a bomb," she said, her eyes showing her adject fear.

"I know, sweetheart. But I'll get you out of this, okay?"

"Okay." She didn't hesitate saying it either, which Hood knew Max appreciated. But she also knew that only put even more pressure on Max.

But Max was doing what Hood was doing: they were searching for that bomb with the clock attached to it that they had seen from outside. And when they saw that they only had ninety-three seconds left, their hearts dropped.

"That's not even two minutes," said Hood.

"DJ's angry with you," Jen said. "He's mad because Daddy died. He blames you."

"I know," Max said. He didn't expect her to refer to Dave Minor as her daddy, but it had been seventeen years. Dave probably told her everything, and probably fed her every lie he could feed her about Max's family too. But Max was too busy looking at those wires. "He won't hurt you ever again," he reassured her as he searched for some kind of way to save her.

"What are we gonna do?" Hood asked him.

Max studied the elaborate bomb. He was getting frantic because he knew there was no time to wait on any bomb squad. Because he knew time was ticking away. From ninety-three seconds to eighty seconds and he hadn't done a damn thing! He didn't know a damn thing to do! There were so many wires. It was nothing like on television where there was a blue wire and a red wire and you had to guess which one. There was a rainbow of wires!

But Hood had gotten down on her back looking at those wires and she suddenly saw an out. "Max, look!"

"I am looking!"

"It's tied to the chair, Max." She got up. "It's tied to the chair!"

"What's tied to the chair?" Max asked, but as soon as he asked it, he realized what Hood meant. He saw where Jen was being held by the straps of the explosive, but the straps were tied to the chair, not to Jen. It was a slim out, but it was all they had.

But he knew, as soon as he tried to move Jen away from those wires, the whole thing could blow. "Leave," he said to Hood.

Hood frowned. "Not without you!"

"Get in the car and go. Get as far away from here as you can get."

"I'm not leaving you, Max."

Max looked at the clock again. Sixty-one seconds. And he knew there was no more time. "I said leave!" he said angrily and grabbed Hood by her arm and ran with her to the basement door.

"Max, don't do this!" she was pleading. "I can help you! Don't do this!"

But no way was Max losing her too. He looked at her with pain in his eyes. "Get as far away from here as you can go. Run for your life, Hood. We'll be okay."

Hood knew he was lying. She knew what he was about to do. "*Max*," she said with pain in her voice and tears in her eyes.

"Just go!" Max yelled at her. And then he pushed her onto the basement stairs and closed and locked the door.

Hood wanted to bang on that door and kick it in. She'd rather die with Max. But she knew Jen needed him. She knew he had no time to waste. And she ran down those basement stairs, ran out of that wall panel, and then ran out through the backyard and around to the side of the house to that window they were able to look into.

And when she saw that clock, and saw that Max only had only forty seconds left, her heart dropped. The thought of leaving Max there didn't even enter her mind. There was no way she was leaving her husband. There was no way!

"Help us, Jesus," she was crying as she ran back around that house, back into that basement, and leaned back and kicked that door open as if she had Herculean strength. And she ran to help Max.

As she was running, Max had already placed his hands beneath Jen's armpits, but every time he tried to move her she touched one of those wires. He was terrified that he was going to trip one of those wires, but he had no choice. He kept trying to lift her body up out of that chair. He glanced at that clock. He had twenty-two seconds left.

Hood saw that clock too and ran to him. "I'll push her up by the bottom of her feet," Hood said, seeing the problem Max was having as soon as she got back inside.

Max had been so focused on getting Jen out of that chair that he didn't even hear her kick the door in. And his heart squeezed in agony that she was going to die with them!

He looked at that clock again.

eleven seconds.

But as soon as Hood grabbed Jen's feet, stabilizing her from the bottom end, Max was able to lift her slender frame without her touching any wires and together they were able to pull Jen out of that chair.

But all three looked at that clock. When they saw that they had only four seconds left, and the clock was suddenly ticking insanely loud as if it was reminding them of their impending doom, too, Max lifted Jen and grabbed Hood and took a few steps, heard the alarm on the clock make a deafening sound, and could do nothing but dive for cover as the bomb did what bombs did and exploded.

Max was on top of Hood, and covered Jen with the rest of his body, as they braced for the impact. Jen was covering her ears because of the sound of the blast, but Max and Hood were praying to God that it wasn't so. That they were not being torn to shreds.

And then there was silence.

They waited. Was this what death sounded like?

Then they realized they weren't torn at all. But the bomb had exploded. They heard the explosion.

Max, stunned, quickly turned toward the bomb. It had exploded, alright, but not on all cylinders. He could see that almost none of the wires had engaged. Could it be possible?

When Hood lifted her head and turned and looked too, she was as stunned as Max. "What happened?"

"It misfired," said Max. Then he smiled and looked at his beautiful wife. "Somehow it misfired!"

Thank you, Jesus!" Hood said with joy in her heart. And Max couldn't agree more.

"But let's get out of here anyway," he said as he helped Jen up, and then he and Hood and Jen hurried out of that home through that basement entry he remembered when he was a wayward kid sneaking out of and then back into the house at night without tripping any alarms.

Once outside, and far away from the house just in case, they could hear police sirens driving up. Emotionally drained, they sat on the lawn.

Jen leaned against her big brother. "They told me you were dead," she said to him.

Max already had his arm around Hood's waist. He placed his other arm around Jen. "They lied to you," he said.

"Daddy treated me okay when we were

in Europe. But every time we came to the States he would never let me go outside. Then when he died, DJ moved me into this place that he said was my childhood home, but I don't remember it."

"That's because it didn't look like this."

"And he would beat on me and make me stay in the basement the whole time we were here. Sometimes he would let me go upstairs. I carved out a peephole one time."

They were grateful for that peephole.

"And then he had Toby make that bomb," said Jen. "I loved Daddy. But I hate DJ."

"He'll never bother you again," Max said.

"You're sure?"

Max nodded. "I'm positive."

Jen nodded too. "I believe you," she said. "You risked your life to save mine. I'll always believe you over anything they said to me."

Max smiled. It was all he could ask for. And he pulled her closer against him.

Then Jen looked at Hood. "Who's that?"

Hood smiled. Max smiled, too, at the way she said it. "That's my wife. Her name is Hood."

"Hood?" asked Jen. "Like a car cover?"

Max smiled at the fact that she didn't go where so many others went. And she said it just right. "Yes" he said as he nodded his head and looked at Hood. "Just like a cover. That's exactly what she is to me. My cover."

And as policemen came running around to the backside of the house, Max and Hood stared into each other's eyes. If she hadn't come back, and he had tripped the wrong wire, that *little* explosion could have killed Jen.

A cover. Exactly right. He could not have described Hood, and what she meant to him, any better.

EPILOGUE

A backyard barbecue and Ricky, with his latest girlfriend by his side, was supposed to be handling the grill-master duties with Max. But Ricky was doing all the work. Max, with a glass of wine in his hand, was too busy standing there enjoying the view.

Rita had a new man too. But this one was worthy of her, Max felt, as he was this gorgeous black chiropractor who could handle a tough lady like Rita. And he treated her like a queen. Except at sports. They were so happily competitive that they were in the pool trying to outstroke each other. Max laughed at how Rita was winning every single lap. Her man tried to pull her back to gain an advantage for himself, but she still won. And they'd laugh about it afterwards.

Rita was no longer a trainee. She was now senior VP and Barkley's boss. And she was already paying off for Max. Projects had never been more on time and under budget than they now were under Rita's stewardship.

Ricky was also excelling in his regional manager role for Max's northeast Cassbars. He was no Rita, because he was just too nice sometimes when firmness was needed, but he was excellent at motivating middle management to get the job done. Max could not have asked for anything more.

Timmy and Jen were even more competitive than Rita and her beau as they did all they could to best each other on the tennis court. You'd think Venus and Serena were playing the way they were grunting and scrambling for every loose ball and laughing as if they were having the time of their lives. They weren't just cousins, but were now inseparable friends who did everything together. Jen, to Max's delight, turned out to be the sweetest young lady they could have ever hoped for despite what she'd been through. She was very childlike as her social growth was badly stunted, and Max had to take on the role of her father rather than her big brother. But he had her in therapy. He wasn't about to minimize what she'd gone through. And she fit right in.

Tish and Jason did too, Max noticed, as he watched them dancing to the old school music blaring out over the stereo system. Neither one of them would win any dance prizes, but Tish had some pretty good moves. But everybody, including Max, wondered if Jason would ever pop the question.

And then he saw Hood. She was seated

on her favorite lounger taking it all in as only Hood knew how to do. Never a big talker, she was an observer. And what she saw, Max could tell, she loved.

As a Tina CD started playing over the stereo, Max grabbed a glass of juice from the tray held by one of their servers, and walked over to his wife. He sat on the side of the lounger next to her lounger and gave her the juice.

"Cheers," he said, and they toasted. "How do you feel?"

"I feel great," Hood said. "Everybody's happy. I'm set."

"And if you're happy," said Max, "I'm happy."

Hood smiled. Then she exhaled. "Tish said that Jason told her that Breena's out."

Max nodded. "She served her six months for her role in Jen's kidnapping all those years ago."

"Where is she?"

"She's back in Prague, her safe haven. I've got a team monitoring her for a while to make sure she's not up to any of her old tricks."

"According to Jen, they treated Breena like a dog," said Hood. "Or worse."

Max nodded. "She was certainly caught up in their madness. Time will tell with her. But

I'm not taking any chances."

Hood appreciated that about Max. He covered his bases. "What was that phone call about?" she asked him.

Max had been on an extended conference call just before he came back outside. "I just got the word. The city council has finally approved my waterfront development deal."

Hood smiled. "For real?"

"For real."

Hood lifted her hand as they high-fived. "You deserve it," she said. "Nobody works harder than you do."

"Rita works hard. I think she has me beat."

Hood couldn't disagree with that. "Except for Rita," she said as she looked over at her sister. "I'm just glad she finally found her somebody decent and who treats her like she should be treated."

"And you work hard too," Max said.

Ever since their action-adventure, Max continued the partnership. He loved her instincts, and the way she observed things he never paid attention to. Every business trip he was on, she was with him, not as his wife, but as his business partner. He was teaching her all the ropes. And she was a fast learner. They were inseparable too.

"And guess what?" Max said.

"What?"

"You're going to be my right-hand man on this development deal project."

Hood smiled again. "Great! But I'll have to work on that."

Max was confused. "Work on what?"

"Being a man."

Max shook his head. "That would classify, my dear, as corny."

Hood laughed. "True that!"

"But isn't it great?" Max asked her.

"Isn't what great?"

"Family. Having one." Then he touched Hood's stomach. "And our baby on the way."

Ever since Hood got the news confirmed from her doctor that she was indeed an expectant mother and three-and-a-half months pregnant, her heart was filled with joy. "Yes. Me a mother? I'm still trying to get over that one."

"Me a father again?" said Max. "Kind of remarkable on both fronts. And you know what else?"

Hood looked at him. "What?"

"There is no one on this planet that I would want to be the mother of my child other than you."

Hood's heart melted, and she couldn't

help herself. She knew Rita wouldn't approve. She knew Rita would declare up and down that she ceded way too much power to Max. But he was her husband, and she was going to give him his due. "Never in a zillion years did I think I'd become somebody's mother," she said. "The very idea used to nauseate me."

Max laughed.

"I'm serious! I've never known anybody good at that job. But knowing you'll be the father, and a very *present* father, eases my mind. Now I can hardly wait."

Max's heart melted too. Hood Riley. His cover.

And that was why, when one of his favorite Tina tunes came over the stereo, he stood up and reached out his hand. "Let's dance on it, Mrs. Cassidy," he said.

Hood gladly stood up, took Max's hand, and right then and there they danced a fast, twirling dance to the Chapman-Knight penned tune:

> "*Simply the best!*
> *Better than all the rest.*
> *Better than anyone.*
> *Anyone I've ever met.*
> *I'm stuck on your heart.*
> *I hang on every word you say.*

Tear us apart?
Baby, I would rather be dead.
Ooh, you're the best!"

Max twirled Hood around with a triple twirl as they laughed as much as they were dancing. Because they were in their own backyard. At their very first get-together. With their little family soon to grow. With their little piece of paradise too.

Visit
mallorymonroebooks.com
and
austinbrookpublishing.com
for more information on all titles.

ABOUT THE AUTHOR

Mallory Monroe is the bestselling author of over one-hundred-and-fifty novels.

Visit

mallorymonroebooks.com

or

austinbrookpublishing.com

or amazon.com/author/mallorymonroe

for more information on all of her titles.

Made in the USA
Middletown, DE
17 February 2023